Dead-Nettle

DEAD-NETTLE

John Buxton Hilton

ST MARTIN'S

NEW YORK

First published in the United States of America in 1977

Library of Congress Cataloging in Publication Data

Hilton, John Buxton
  Dead-nettle

  I. Title
PZ4.H6568Db3 [PR6058.15] 823'.9'14   77–160

ISBN: 0 312 18500 6

Printed in Great Britain by
THE ANCHOR PRESS LTD
Tiptree, Essex

Bound in Great Britain by
WM BRENDON & SON LTD
Tiptree, Essex

CHAPTER ONE

Hetty Wilson was five days in Derby: long enough to make her mark. But it was not clear what sort of mark she had made. She had not actually caused trouble, merely caused trouble to be anticipated. No one wanted to admit having seen her: which was predictable. Even Constable Kewley was not anxious to talk about her. Yet she must certainly have passed him that night as he nosed his way between St Mary's Gate and St Helen's – just as she must have passed Tilly Sutcliffe and Martha Lang under the archway of Harriman's oil-store. It was equally sure that these two were waiting for her to trip over the toe of an accidentally extended clog. A loop of leather thong was round Martha Lang's wrist, under the hanging corner of her tatty shawl. And Duncan Mottershead was watching her from across the street, leaning on the wall of Hindley's shop, his bowler-hat tilted across his eye-brows, but too grease-stained to be rakish, his right hand in his trouser pocket, grasping as always the comfort of an old sock stuffed with sand.

It was difficult to know what Hetty Wilson had actually done in Derby. She had not picked up any men, though she had been injudicious with her smiles. That, perhaps, was what had primed the defensive network. Certain sections of Derby society in 1905 were hyper-sensitive.

There had been a preposterous rustic flavour about her appearance when first she arrived in town, though it is difficult to know whom she was trying to fool. Herself, perhaps? She came obviously from the easy-going south – she spoke with a regional accent which was resented in and around St Mary's Gate, but which people could not precisely place. Perhaps she thought she was coming amongst a community of musical comedy rustics. Her hair hung beside her ears in cork-screw ringlets and her bodice was laced across her bosom as if she had just stepped from a stage chorus of *Robin Hood*, the vivid green of her blouse in aggressive contrast to the crushed strawberry of her sweeping skirts – all in provocative disharmony with the chipped chocolate paint of the scabrous boarding-house for which she made an inexplicable bee-line. Yet there was something about Hetty Wilson in which the observer, against his better judgement, was tempted to believe. It could have derived from her effortlessly healthy complexion, the natural perfection of her skin, the clarity of her eyes. She was in her mid-twenties, but did not have to do much work upon herself to appear eighteen.

A striking figure, yet they wanted me to believe that they had forgotten her in the hinterland of St Mary's. I had to waste a good deal of time talking to people who were loth to linger in my company. Fortunately their memories were clearer and less inhibited about the man with the surgical boot whose route I picked up from the Midland Station, across the Market Place and along Irongate. I eventually established that Hetty Wilson had presented herself at Emma Rice's boarding-house as if she knew exactly where she was coming. She had paid a week's rent in advance without demur, not even attempting to haggle over Emma's first demand. Moreover, having installed herself, and changed into

6

clothes barely distinguishable, though cleaner, than the amorphous folds of Tilly Sutcliffe and Martha Lang, she had not demonstrated any obvious reason for being here at all. She had neither looked for nor enquired after work. It was true that she had a way of looking at men that disturbed their regular circle of women – but she had shown an equal skill at not allowing things to develop any further. She gave an impression of robust determination, but it took the form for the time being of conscious patience. Hetty Wilson was waiting for something to happen. Presumably it had to do with the visits that she made twice daily to the *Poste Restante* counter at the General Post Office.

Three times a stranger to the town came looking for her, a gentleman on the fringe of early middle life who had the ill luck to miss her on each occasion by the narrowest of margins. Once, indeed, he came so close that she had to engage herself in a labyrinth of tenement yards and private alley-ways. In the arts of evasion she showed herself to be a resourceful woman. At last an almost successful *coup* brought the gentleman to the very door of Emma Rice's, but Emma disclaimed all knowledge of her. That must have cost Hetty Wilson supplementary rent.

Perhaps it was money that she was waiting for at the General Post Office. But for the first few days nothing came, and choosing an unfrequented moment, she pawned for two guineas at Hindley's a fifteen carat bracelet, inset with oriental pearls. It must have been worth every penny of five.

She was not known to have spent any of this money. She did not linger by the shop-fronts on her way from the Post Office. And on the morning of the sixth day she came away from the counter with a small white envelope, which she tore open in a corner of the public

7

concourse, apparently not bearing to wait until she was out in the street again.

She returned rapidly to her lodgings, remained out of sight until the middle of the evening, and then re-appeared before the public eye once more in her crushed strawberry and green, running the gauntlet of Duncan Mottershead, Martha Lang and Tilly Sutcliffe, strategic-ally placed in the shadows cast by a wheezing gas-light. She also passed very close to Constable Kewley, who kept his back resolutely turned to her as he peered un-convincingly through the slats of a venetian blind into the darkness of a shop interior.

Kewley, a hardened constable whose peace and comfort depended on the local balance of power, then moved unobtrusively away. Hetty Wilson, side-stepping to avoid a dollop of horse-droppings that had got itself by no accident on to the pavement, was intended to trip over the toe-cap of Tilly Sutcliffe's boot, and an alter-cation was then envisaged during which Martha Lang would reveal, perhaps even use, the thong at her wrist. Duncan Mottershead would then, in exaggeratedly leisurely fashion, untip himself from his leaning-post and amble across the road, reassuring himself that the sand-bag in his pocket was ready for action. He would intervene in the rising strife, staying the hands of the two well rehearsed women with a blunt syllable or two. About what might have happened next, I can only speculate. Hetty Wilson might have been invited to accept Duncan Mottershead's protection or to betake her rustic charms elsewhere. It could have been a plain intended case of robbery with violence. I have not been able to discover that there was any particular reason why matters should have come to a head that evening. There are a number of things that continue to puzzle me. I do not know – though I can venture a few guesses –

8

how Mottershead and his henchwomen were aware that Hetty Wilson was going to leave Emma Rice's precisely when she did. I cannot discover that she herself had done anything to precipitate their decision. Perhaps by now she had merely succeeded in out-waiting her antagonists. Her patience, for whatever purpose she was exercising it, had become too much for their nerves. She was slow to show her hand, so they felt compelled to call it.

But things did not work out in that way. Tilly's foot was already out and Hetty tripped over it. But Martha did not uncurl her thong and Mottershead continued to lean against the wall as if he were an indifferent spectator of forthcoming events. Into the orbit of the hissing gas-lamp, down the very middle of the road-way, side-stepping as if he were uncertain whether to allow a brougham to pass, or to stop horse and carriage with the small of his back, another figure was approaching. His air of purpose was unambiguous.

He was a big man, aged perhaps on the young side of thirty and he had a full ring of beard about his neck and chin in the countryman's manner, though his cheeks were cleanly shaven. There was a hint of clumsy and suppressed strength about his gait, his arms swinging idly, huge hands hanging loosely like paper bags stuffed with chestnuts: an awesome opponent, but one who looked too slow and lethargic to fight willingly. The only part of him that did not appear relaxed was his left leg, which was stiff at the knee, and which needed a positive effort for every step forward, since it was hampered by a large and unshapely surgical boot.

Hetty Wilson gave a spontaneous yelp of delight at the sight of him, ran up to him with unathletic, mincing steps, put her hands on his shoulders and kissed him warmly on the cheek. But he seemed impervious to her proximity. He looked down at her without a smile, without, as far as the by-standers could make out, a word of any kind. The look on his face gave nothing away to strangers. He might have been angry with her, he might have been tacitly exasperated, his stony features might have been asking her an unspoken question. The one reaction which he did not display was joy to match her own. A baker's journeyman cursed them from the box-seat of his van as he reined aside to avoid them. They took a step out of the way and almost fell foul of a rag-and-bone man's cart that was coming from the opposite direction. Then, when the road was clear, the man took the woman's wrists and removed her hands from his shoulders. They walked together back to Emma Rice's, from where they very quickly re-emerged, the man carrying the woman's Gladstone bag. He put the flat of his hand against her shoulder-blade, but it was to thrust her forward, not to impart personal assurance. She walked obediently beside him, adjusting the rhythm of her steps to his with difficulty, but finding his natural pace after the first few yards.

Duncan Mottershead and his pair of women remained where they were, taking no ostensible interest. But when Hetty Wilson and her escort were out of sight, Mottershead came away from his wall and without looking at the women strolled in the direction of the *Feathers*. They adjusted their shawls about their elbows and walked away, making no effort to join him.

And these were the people who afterwards claimed to be unaware of Hetty Wilson's existence. But Hetty Wilson, that evening, was on her way to a violent death. They therefore had to be helped to remember.

It was not too difficult; it merely took time, and time was what I did not have enough of. I knew Martha Lang, Tilly Sutcliffe and Duncan Mottershead at least as well as they thought they knew me. There were little things about them that it had always suited me to keep in reserve – things that as far as I was concerned could remain in the shadows, as long as they co-operated when I needed them. But first I had to brow-beat Constable Kewley.

'This woman, Kewley – you hadn't said a word about her to your Sergeant, or to Inspector Bramwell.'

'I'd no call to, Inspector Brunt. She didn't look as if she was breaking any laws.'

'That's beside the point.' How often I had tried to impress upon the uniformed branch that any morsel of gossip might one day fill a breach.

'And you were within twenty yards of an impending affray. You were actually edging away from it.'

'I was ready to blow my whistle.'

'Your whistle!'

'You know how it is, Inspector. A lot happened that night. A horse laid down and died in Edward Street. A lady's dog was set upon by mongrels. But I think I'm beginning to remember this other woman now, sir.'

'You'd better.'

I hoped he knew that it didn't matter to me how he organised his beat. He didn't have to hedge his bets for my sake. But I wanted facts, and I didn't want to take ten minutes wheedling them out of him. I was angry with him, but I was keeping it strictly unofficial. Old Kewley was too good a bobby to be alienated across a strip of carpet. Things seldom went badly on his strip – and he knew exactly what was a fair price to pay for the King's Peace.

'I reckoned her a tart,' he said. 'From away. And about to be warned off, with no harm done. Which would have saved us all a lot of trouble. The only thing – '

'Yes?'

'She'd been keeping out of somebody else's way. An outsider.'

'Not Clubfoot?'

'No. She went up to Clubfoot openly. She was glad to see him. She seemed to expect that he'd feel the same about her.'

'But he didn't?'

'He didn't seem to know what to make of her. Or of himself, at that moment.'

'And this other chap?'

'Ex military, I'd say – or a flat-catcher trying to look like one.'

'And not a Derby man?'

'For sure he's not. Staying at the *Bell Inn*. Gone now, of course.'

'We'll be knowing where. In the meantime, anything that comes to your ears had better come to mine.'

Of the possible informants, I chose Tilly Sutcliffe. I had reasons for thinking she might be the easiest of the three. I bought her an unexpected port and lemon in the *Seven Stars*. She was a simple soul, incapable of maintaining a consistent lie, but not even easily upset when you'd up-arsed her lack of logic. She weighed up a free drink against the tarnishing of her reputation by being seen talking to the likes of me. The port and lemon won; that was the measure of Tilly Sutcliffe.

She knew nothing about anyone; was daft enough to include Hetty Wilson in her general declaration of innocence, even though I had not yet mentioned the woman. So I started talking whimsically about Marjorie Haddon; she could hardly pretend ignorance of Marjorie.

'Just a little matter of supplying what is called, in the Offences against the Person Act of 1861, *a noxious thing*.'

We didn't trouble ourselves much about successful

abortions and, God knows, in Marjorie Haddon's case I wouldn't have wanted to. But Tilly paled.

'I'd rather talk about Hetty Wilson, though,' I said.

'We can do without her sort here. God's gift to married men – she thought.'

'Who, in particular?'

'No one in particular, Mr Brunt.'

Of course not.

'But she didn't keep her eyes to herself. She was taking her time, if you ask me. She had money – some – but it wasn't going to last for ever. Emma Rice had driven a tight bargain, and she'd had to raise the second week's rent on a bangle. After that, I reckon she'd have been back on a job she was no stranger to. But she seemed to be wanting to hold off as long as she could. She was waiting for something through the post. It came – and she went.'

Tilly got on to the subject of the lame man and was keen to concentrate my attention on him. She must have been relieved that I did not mention Marjorie Haddon again.

One way or another, Tilly Sutcliffe provided me with most of the details, some of them speculative, I know, which I have chronicled so far. In point of fact, most of it did not help me much. Yet it confirmed a few things, which made it worth while. It is always useful to have one's guess-work reinforced.

But I wasn't led from Derby to the man with the surgical boot. It was the man with the surgical boot who had led me to Derby.

Corpses do not usually bother me, but I had already heard some striking descriptions of Hetty Wilson in her prime. They contrasted savagely with the purple pulp that somebody had made of her.

CHAPTER TWO

Like grand opera, this story has a recurring *leitmotif* : a series of unannounced arrivals.

In the manner of most men who have come great distances, Frank Lomas fetched up at his destination early in the evening – a fresh and pleasant evening in September 1904, some six months previous to the appearance of Hetty Wilson in the less salubrious back streets of Derby. One of several odd things about him was that though he had never set foot in the place before, it was abundantly clear that Margreave was his considered destination. There had been a paradoxical quickening of his steps as he set himself at the last long hill into the organic grey stone huddle of the town, a broad smile amidst the halo of beard as he sank with a pewter tankard on to an uncushioned settle, having assured himself of a room at the *Adventurers' Arms*. He looked at people as if he thought that by some miracle they ought to have been expecting him. This, however, was far from the case. He was given the impression that most of those he had met were reluctant to make his acquaintance. Margreave was not fond of strangers.

The town was an amorphous cluster of slate-roofed limestone cottages, its streets laid out according to no plan, a once prosperous, now barely even interesting settlement in what is known as the Low Peak, an area much less attractive to tourists than the dales to the north and west, not served by main routes through the county and no longer an object of curiosity except to industrial historians.

Frank Lomas was manifestly not welcome, though he had achieved this goal at the end of a pilgrimage of some six and a half thousand miles. The Peakrels are an unforthcoming and unself-revealing community, and in the case of Margreave in the opening years of this century, this was exacerbated because the more outward looking and ambitious of the male population had long since departed to earn elsewhere a more substantial living than these hills could afford them. Of those that remained, most worked in the limestone quarries or the kilns; a few scraped the parlous soil for a reward that scarcely fobbed off starvation. Their instinct was to distrust the unfamiliar and more especially to conceal, even from each other, the fact that they were capable of any human feeling other than a mute stoicism. I, too, had suffered from their sullen silences when first I had been drafted into this area. Frank Lomas found it particularly hard to understand; he had learned to survive by cocking a snook at privation. Not so these men. They laughed occasionally, but only amongst themselves. They were capable of personal loyalties and a sustained battle against their environment. But they would rather lay claim to a twisted motivation than confess to a candid one. Your Peakrel does not wear his heart upon his sleeve; he prefers the fiction that he has no heart at all.

And Frank Lomas had several characteristics which the men of Margreave found unendearing. He was, for one thing, openly inquisitive. On his way up the last hill, the last short lap of his journey, he had paused to take an interest in a drainage channel from one of the abandoned lead workings in the flank of Ranters' Hill. And he had no right to be taking an interest in derelict mines. They were essentially the heritage of Margreave men. Later, when the main oracular force of the *Adventurers'* had gathered for the evening, he had had the temerity to ask his neighbour at the bar some

questions to which he seemed to expect specific answers
– questions about the present state of mining in the
district. It was a dangerous subject on which to display
curiosity; to the Peakrel, the desire for knowledge might
all too easily seem the first step towards unfair advantage. Indeed, they were already beginning to believe
that this man must be something of a fool into the
bargain. It was fifty years or more since anyone had
endeavoured to tear any sort of living from the mineral
deposits in Margreave's four hills.

But there was another failing which, more than any
other, caused the men of Margreave to combine in tele-
pathic accord against Frank Lomas. He already knew a
good deal more about their town than could possibly be
healthy. He seemed as familiar with Margreave's by-
ways and personalities as if he had already lived here
half his life. He referred to Mrs Bassett, the acidulous
postmistress, as Old Fan. He knew old Tiggy Slack by
name and nickname before either had been spoken in his
presence. Yet he made mistakes, too. He thought that
Edward Fothergill was still Bar Master of the Moot
Court, whereas the old man had died five years ago. He
spoke of old Edward as if he had been a shining example
of the probity of the previous century, whereas things
had come to light about some of the Fothergill trans-
actions that made a plain villain of anyone who spoke
in his favour. Men began to talk pointedly to each other
in low voices and to exclude Frank Lomas from their
conversation. But he persevered.

'Is Dead-Nettle Drift being worked these days?'

'Dead-Nettle?'

There was a stir of interest, even amongst those who
had turned their backs on him.

'Dead-Nettle Drift? The man who works Dead-Nettle
might well take his time over his last square meal.'

'I'd not take Dead-Nettle if you paid the Lord's Seam for me before I hung my outside door.'

'There must be lead left in these hills,' Lomas said.

'Aye – lead – copper and silver too, if you'd like to take a reading-glass to what you find. There's lead aplenty. Enough to see this country's muskets through another war, if ever need be. And water, too. That's been the curse of all time in the Margreave mines. Who can afford a pumping-engine, on top of the royalties? Do you know how the Lord's Seam works, lad? Do you know what flogging dead horse means? Working for the mineral owner's rights, and hoping she won't flood before you strike your pick into another scrin that they'll let you call your own.'

'The Moot Court still meets, then?'

'The Moot Court *exists*. There's a Master and a Steward and a standing jury, if only to pass judgement on Florence Belfield's ghosts. Thinking of working the Drift, were you? You wouldn't fill your freeing-dish with what's left in Dead-Nettle. There's nowt left in Dead-Nettle, only toad-stone.'

A surprising spate of fluency. Lomas did his best to exploit it.

'So who owns the manor now? I'm told there's a new landlord.'

'And I'd starve on crusts before I put a penny into that bugger's bank. Not that it matters who's owner of the land. You fill your dish, and you've the right to work the seam as long as there's work left in you. That's the law of the liberty.'

A strange sort of excitement had come over them. It was fifty years since the ore had been seriously worked. There were not many here who could ever have taken an active hand at the rock-face. But the talk had roused some spirit in them.

'And for all that's just been said, those would be the last of my reasons for not working Dead-Nettle. It's a bad luck gate. Always has been.'

'Aye.'

And even Frank Lomas, for all his monumental simplicity of outlook, knew better than to press the point any further.

'You're a miner, then?' somebody asked him.

'I have been in my time. Not lead, though.'

'You have been in your time? Why, you're nobbut a lad.'

But there was no pressing interest in his history.

'Coal,' he volunteered.

'Oh, aye?' and a contemptuous echo from the spittoon.

'You'll find no coal up round here.'

'I know that. If I did, I'd run ten miles.'

'Run, would you?'

The man cast his eyes down at Lomas's surgical boot. Perhaps that was the beginning of their hostility. A surgical boot made a man different, and no man had a right to be different.

Perhaps I seem less than charitable to the Margreave men. Perhaps I am prejudiced; it has more than once fallen to my lot to rely on such frankness as I could cajole from them. If ever they wanted to outwit me, I was outwitted. Maybe they could rise to selflessness, sacrifice, even bravery, under the right kind of persuasion. I suppose there might even be circumstances under which they could be tolerant of what they do not understand. But on this theoretical point I remain unconvinced. Frank Lomas found them perplexing; but at bottom he did not care whether they – or any other man – understood him or not.

The morning after his arrival, he was busy in the

village in a manner which suggested a plan drawn up beforehand. He went first and looked in the window of Tiggy Slack's Stores in the grey, sloping Market Place: chopped firewood, pots of jam, sides of bacon, lamp-wicks and canisters of tea. It had been a lesson of Lomas's youth, one of his father's adages, that when you were faced with half a dozen jobs to do, you squared up first to the one that you had the least taste for. He looked in through the panels of the shop-door, saw Tiggy Slack, the man he had identified last night, a balding stoat of a figure, plunging a metal scoop into a bin of rice. He was serving a round-shouldered, black-weeded widow; excuse enough for Lomas to postpone his visit. He went instead to a white-washed Queen Anne house at the lower end of the Square, where the footpath became so steep that it devolved into a flight of stone steps protected by a hand-rail.

He was told by a housekeeper to wait in a cold, stone-flagged hall. Five minutes later Isaac Grundy, Bar Master, appeared and took him into an equally cold parlour. Lomas's impression was that the Bar Master knew of his errand without needing to be told. But he tried to behave as if he had no inkling what it was all about, waited for Lomas to tell him; a clean but fragile old man, with owl-like round lenses in nickel-framed spectacles.

'Dead-Nettle Drift? You're talking of freeing the Drift?'

'That's why I'm here.'

The old man went to his sideboard and took from it a register bound in scuffed leather, its entries dating back to the seventeenth century. He sought out a line with his forefinger, though he must surely have known the last hundred years of the liberty by heart.

'Dead-Nettle hasn't been worked since the 1830s. You know the law?'

Lomas nodded.

'Fill the dish. And I shall want to see some evidence that there really is a seam. No salting it, no faking. Prove you're into a seam, and yours is the right to work it.'

'I know that.'

'You must put a door on and keep the quarter area in safe and respectable repair.'

'I'll do that.'

Grundy looked over the top of his spectacles. 'There'll be a rent to pay. It was fixed three hundred years ago. A groat a year: four pence. You pay that to the Steward.'

'I'll see to it.'

Grundy was about to close the book, but allowed his eye to run over the rest of the page.

'There isn't a working in the liberty but's waiting to be freed. You can take free choice. You can dig any-where bar the churchyard or in a man's orchard; which needn't trouble you, since no man here has an orchard. You could let the water out of Murchison's Swallet with a month's hard work. There's a vein down there that could keep you busy for years.'

'I fancy Dead-Nettle.'

'That's your affair, then. You know it's a stope?'

Lomas didn't, but pretended that he did. Grundy was not fooled.

'A stope – the cavity from a worked-out vein. There was an outlying scrin in Dead-Nettle, almost an out-crop. And when it was done, it was done.'

'I'll drive deeper. Happen there's another seam.'

'Then your first job is to collect your showing. When you've got it up, I'll open the Court House and get out the dish.'

'Yes, Mr Grundy.'

Grundy moved towards the door of his parlour.

'I shall be wanting lodgings in the town,' Lomas said. 'If you know anyone who might have a room to spare?'

'You weren't thinking of quartering up at the Drift, then?'

'I'm no man for my creature comforts, Bar Master, but I've had my fill of hard lying.'

'There's a cottage at Dead-Nettle,' Grundy said, making no reference to his ignorance of the point. 'And in a mess. But a man like you could make it habitable in a couple of weeks.'

'Maybe.'

'Go and see Esmond Fuller about it. He's the new land-lord – bought Margreave Hall a year and a half ago; though God knows why. I don't think he'd jib at accept-ing a shilling or two of rent.'

'I was going to see him anyway, about the mine.'

'No need for that. The mine is the concern of the Moot Court.'

'I know, but it's only good manners.'

Grundy let him out. There was gratifying freshness in the air of the Market Place after the dankness of Grundy's front room.

This time he did not shirk his confrontation with Tiggy Slack, pushed open the door of the shop, which set in motion a hand-bell. There were two other customers, and a tomato-faced woman, possibly his wife, was helping Slack to serve. Lomas waited his turn. The atmosphere was an amalgam of coffee and tallow candles, of smoked bacon and paraffin, of old cheese and soap. It reminded Lomas of something from his own past. The red-faced woman was speaking to him.

'Yes?'

'I was wanting a private word with Mr Slack.'

The man looked at him sideways. The bell announced yet another customer.

'You can see that I'm busy.'

'It isn't on my own account. I was asked to deliver a message.'

Slack looked at him sceptically. The woman turned her eyes on him again, then looked anxiously at Slack. She was his wife, then.

'So what is it?'

'In private, if that's at all possible.'

Lomas talked like a man of good manners, prepared to be patient. Slack had been weighing flour. He brushed his hands together and took Lomas behind the counter into an office where there was only room for a roll-top desk and a man to sit at it. There was a litter of ledgers, an open day-book, stacks of coins counted out in the lid of a meat-cube tin.

'Well?'

'It's some months now since I saw him, but I am to tell you that Gilbert is well.'

'We know no Gilbert here.'

He said it like a bad actor declaiming the would-be key-line of a hackneyed melodrama. At the same time, he glared at Lomas with all the theatrical hatred he could muster. He was speaking figuratively, of course, but what he said was meant to be final. Lomas looked back at him with unaffected calm.

'That was the message. I have done what I was asked to.'

Slack stretched over to open the office door, pinned with wholesaler's price-lists and proprietary calendars. Then he had an additional thought.

'So now we know who's filled your mind with Dead-Nettle Drift.'

'I shall be working Dead-Nettle Drift according to the letter of the usages.'

'No doubt. We can do without the likes of you in Margreave,' Slack said.

And thereupon Lomas closed the door behind him with his elbow, pushed Slack gently in the chest with the flat of his hand, yet firmly enough to catch him off balance and jam him against the side of the desk. Then he pinched the little man's nose between his thumb and forefinger, giving it a little tweak, insulting rather than painful.

'I could mention one or two uncomfortable little spots where Gilbert and I have been. And the likes of you ought to be glad of it.'

He plunged out of the shop, not waiting for Slack to collect himself, not lingering to learn Mrs Slack's reaction, though her hand reached out to try to touch his sleeve.

And how is it that I am able to record all this in such intimate detail? Because before I was finished it fell to my lot to tease the memories of a lot of people in Margreave, including Isaac Grundy and the Slacks. Most telling of all, I was closeted for long hours with Frank Lomas. That is an aspect of a policeman's work that is sometimes overlooked by the public at large. Sudden shafts of intuition can be very impressive; so are strokes of luck and an eye for anomalous details. But the most memorable, to my mind, of all the cases that I have ever broken have depended on the long, patient build-up of confidence in some essentially lonely man. Often it has been confidence unfairly gained and falsely sustained. Equally commonly I have betrayed him the moment the climax was won. Yet I would not call myself a ruthless man; sometimes I fear I am in danger of becoming a mere sentimentalist. But that can help, too. It sometimes leads me into temporary sympathy with men even more sentimental than myself. And if a man will commit murder for anything other than material gain, he must be sentimental indeed.

When he left Slack's shop, Frank Lomas made his way directly up to Dead-Nettle Drift. He knew exactly where the mine was. There were things that he knew about Margreave in mind-shattering detail. But there were other things that he did not know at all. And certain other aspects he had worked out in his imagination, sometimes with remarkable felicity. But often he was ludicrously wide of the mark, too.

So Dead-Nettle Drift, though he knew exactly where it was, came as an initial shock to him. Situated on a waste corner of the Margreave Hall estate, it was visible for a torturing time before he succeeded in reaching it : an ashen gash in the hill-side, a neglected chute of waste and rubble, a partially ruined hovel, a minimal cluster of out-buildings. He had to plod through a bowl of deceptive dead ground, ankle-sucking bog and reed-bed. It promised badly for the drainage of the mine itself. When he had finally scrambled up the waste-tip, his unrelieved impression was of dereliction and sterility. He picked up a handful of cat dirt – the miner's name for decayed and crumbling rock-refuse – and saw that there was indeed a glint here and there of galena, lead sulphide, the basic mineral. He picked at its bed of calcite with his finger-nail and was left with a sliver of ore that would have been lost in a thimble.

Frank Lomas is basically an uncompromising man – stern with himself, strongly moved by copy-book aphorisms and chapel texts. He unshakably believes that the moment of deepest discouragement is the one that most calls for astringent rededication. He is an almost uncrushable optimist which is, and has been at every cross-roads of his life, the source of his most bitter tragedies. He let the gritty cat dirt fall over the toe of his boot and moved over to look at the living quarters. It was a limestone cottage, the door missing, the windows long broken, the damp plaster rotting from the inside walls. A ladder, which needed replacement, served as a staircase up to a floor divided into two bedrooms, one very small. There were slates missing from the roof, their fragments lying on the slag-heap below. A fortnight, three weeks, a month, to make the place barely habitable, before he even started to work on his dish?

Behind the house was a shippon for a couple of cows, a rough pasture, less than a quarter of an acre, marked out by a dry-stone wall conspicuous for the gaps in it, a bin, rusted into holes, that had once contained corn. You couldn't call the place a farm, hardly even a small-holding. But the hills of the Low Peak are scattered with such miserable agricultural parcels. They were the miner's attempt to eke out the thinness of his ore with an equally treacherous hope of subsistence.

Lomas walked into the entrance to the mine itself. A drift is a horizontal, or almost horizontal channel driven into the surface rock. Dead-Nettle went down at an angle of thirty degrees for some sixty feet, culminating in two lateral galleries, neither more than ten feet in depth, hacked out obliquely from the main heading: an unfinished cross-cut. There was little evidence of ore in the walls: one dark patch hardly as big as his head. As Grundy had said: a stope. The vein – it might originally have been a substantial one – was worked out.

But more might be found. The hills were full of it. There might be a parallel stratum, a basset, below this. A trial-shaft here, a cross-probe there. Frank Lomas was committed. He was a man who thought and walked in straight lines and went through obstacles rather than round them. And was there not, besides, the evidence of Gilbert Slack? The night that Gilbert had told him of Dead-Nettle Drift, he wasn't telling lies. They had both been too near their Maker in the hours that preceded that dawn to want to take chances with their immortal souls.

He set out towards Margreave Hall.

CHAPTER THREE

A mock Palladian cube, a façade of pilasters and balconettes and false balustrades that gave the impression of little more depth than if it had all been painted direct on the dour stonework. I tried to tap Lomas's reactions, when he came to tell me of his first visit to Margreave Hall; it fascinated me to know whether he had some streak of instinctive aesthetic taste which might lead him, off guard, to some gem of summary judgement. The place might have over-awed him by its size and by its pretensions to antiquity; or he might have held it in contempt for reasons of sour-grape politics, or even through some true vein – some scrin, basset or pipe – of genuine values.

He disappointed me. He had walked into the place taking it as he saw it, and had not thought about it at all; the den of the lion he was about to beard, no more. He had heard in the inn the previous evening of the adverse feeling of the community against the man who had bought the manorial rights. Did this affect the spirit in which he approached the new châtelain? I think not. I think that Frank Lomas was only ever affected by two considerations: the job currently in hand, and the possibility that somewhere, someone or other might have taught him an epigram that assessed, clarified and disposed of the whole situation.

He passed fallen statuary, Arcadian youths with chipped noses in lichen-crusted shifts, prone with their curvaceous arms and stringless bows amongst the seeded grasses of neglected lawns. Wild thyme luxuriated amongst the massive amphora of a weathered terrace, sowthistles lorded it in the crevices between flag-stones. But it was the confusion of partial repair, not the chaos of decay. Everything was progressing towards new order, not running downhill to final dilapidation. The area around an Augustan belvedere had been weeded and swept clean, a barrow laden with sere nettles, teasles and wilting white goosefoot waiting to be wheeled behind the scenes. But no one was in evidence to do the wheeling.

Lomas found the portentous front door open and there was no answer to his tug at the bell. He went in and looked about himself, as far as he could manage it without vulgar curiosity, expecting to meet someone at any moment. Behind a door at the other end of the mock-Adam hall, a quarrel seemed to be in progress: a man's voice, confident but exasperated, and a woman's, fluent, emphatic – and amused.

'Pray, then, for a radical Tory or a paternalist Leveller. It matters not what name you give him. If he calls himself one thing, and then does the other, he shall perhaps have the votes of us all.'

'Or none,' the woman said.

'And the Co-operative Movement shall live by the Wealth of Nations.'

Lomas tapped on the panel of the door, and when there was no reply, was about to try once again before penetrating further. But as he raised his hand, the door was torn open in his face. The woman, who could not have heard him, was striding out of the room and pulled herself up so close in front of him that he stepped back in confusion. She was laughing – not at him, but at the discussion in which she had just been involved – and which must therefore have been lacking in the acrimony that Lomas had ascribed to it. She was a woman of about Lomas's age, dressed for morning country visiting, gloves in her hand, natural dark curls peeping neatly under her hat, the image of the immaculate and untouchable.

'Please be so kind as to lower your knuckles,' she said. 'You look as if you're about to hit me. And I'm not sure that I fancy gentle persuasion from that particular hand.'

Lomas told me that the moment reminded him of an encounter he had had once with the daughter of his Adjutant, on home-station, in a red-brick barracks built at the time of the Crimea. They had both been in some measure out of bounds: he in the shade of a kitchen-garden behind the officers' mess, to which he had gone to steal privacy; she, like as not, on the way to an assignation with a subaltern. The shock of coming upon each other round a sudden corner threw them both into an instant of unguarded intimacy. He had looked directly into her eyes and smiled; she had looked back at him – and had been the first to collect herself. She pouted – weak lips that sank at the corners – and though he had stood well aside to let her pass, she had gathered up a handful of her skirt as if she feared contamination. Later, she had complained to her father that he had accosted her with dumb insolence; he had been awarded

28

confinement for fourteen days without the option.

But outside the door of the morning room of Margreave Hall he looked into Isobel Fuller's eyes and she did not divert them.

'You have some business with my father?'

Two encounters with women : both differing mightily from his first meeting with Hetty Wilson.

For the moment Isobel Fuller stood looking at him, a light of not unkindly amusement still playing in her eyes. She then stood aside and swept her arm in the direction of her father, who was sitting in a chair by the window overlooking the terrace. She appeared almost to be making Lomas a present of him.

Lomas went in and was asked to sit down, clumsily conscious of his boots on the parquet. He explained his business, and Fuller listened with the occasional interruption of a brief and acute question.

'Well, it seems to me, Mr Lomas, that the laws and customs of this locality give me no choice. I simply must sit back and allow you to add to my income with no contribution on my part in any shape or form. The prospect pleases me immensely. I shall of course have to face a bitter scene with my vicious Radical of a daughter for not waiving my rights to a share in your takings. But I assure you that no man shall ever find me guilty of such weakness. It is not by feeble-minded generosity that I have been able to buy myself everything but ancestors.'

I do not know whether Lomas understood this as embittered irony, or whether he thought it idiosyncratic plutocracy at its face value. Possibly he was so innured to eccentricities in his superiors that he had the habit of ignoring them. Esmond Fuller was an elderly man whose bodily chemicals had preserved in him an appearance of lean austerity, even at the height of his

29

evident prosperity. He made a sort of mock heroism out of sharp business dealing, implying shameless guilt of all those malpractices which, in a life of almost unvaried success, he had undoubtedly shunned at whatever cost to himself. I do not know whether Lomas was subtle-minded enough to see this. What matters is that he immediately and thenceforward liked the old man, whether he understood him or not. And the old man – whose understanding of Lomas was, I think, consummate from the start – evidently took to him at once.

'You may think that I am a heartless capitalist, a combination of Shylock and Scrooge, though unrelieved by the more endearing qualities of either. I should go on thinking that, if I were you. You will find it an umbrella against ultimate disillusion. But remember that if I reach out for my percentage whilst you burst your arteries at the rock-face, I am still only being paid for the labours of my younger years.'

'Yes, sir.'

Lomas broached the question of the Dead-Nettle cottage.

'I know, of course, the ruin that you mention. You are telling me that that too might become a source of unearned income to me?'

'I know I can make something of it.'

'Three shillings and fourpence a week,' the old man said. 'Paid in advance, and any improvements are your own concern and liability.'

And Fuller looked down at the surgical boot.

'That isn't going to interfere with your work in enclosed spaces?'

'It never interferes with anything I want to do.'

'An accident?'

'A Boer bullet. It took away the calf muscle – or, at least, the army surgeons did. It has shortened my leg, because the heel is permanently raised. That's why the boot is four soles thick.'

'At Colenso, was this?'

'At Vaal Krantz. But I had been at Colenso too.'

The old man had a patriot's expertise in even minor skirmishes of the South African War.

'General Buller made me a Queen's Corporal in the field after Colenso,' Lomas said, naturally and unboastfully. Fuller's admiration was genuine.

'But don't try to live on it, young man. There are troubles waiting for you in Dead-Nettle Drift, I am sure. But I don't think you'll meet many Boers in there.'

Later, when Lomas was crossing the room to go, Fuller called him back.

'I'll leave you to regularise all the mining matters with Grundy. I don't run to an agent, so I have to do most things for myself. I'll draw up an agreement about the cottage and send it round for you to sign. In the meantime, I hope you will let me know from time to time how things go. I'm making no promises, but there might come a time when a modest investment could save work for you and make money for me. There are two kinds of interest, and I need both of them. One you take *from* a job, one you take *in* it. I'm finding that a park full of broken statues leaves me bored most of the time.'

Lomas passed those statues again on his way back into town. But his eyes were scanning all horizons more keenly for any signs of the woman who had laughingly accused him of raising his fist to her. She was nowhere in sight; only tall elms, their leaves already veined with incipient orange after a dry late summer. In a field a man to whom Lomas had talked in the *Adventurers' Arms* was spreading stable muck with slow rhythmic sweeps of a two-pronged fork. He did not look away

31

from his work to notice Lomas's passing. But after Lomas had passed, the man leaned on his fork and looked steadily after him.

CHAPTER FOUR

Isobel Fuller was disturbed, if not actually worried about her father. It had all been so unfair, the early retirement after the economic heart-searching; the house and grounds that did nothing for him, though they would have done everything for the pair if her mother had lived. As it was, she had died between the signing of the conveyance and the arrival of the first batch of workmen to make the place habitable. Her father had tried to sustain his interest but, utterly unlike himself, had flitted from task to task and finished none of them. And she had some inkling of his other disappointments, though he kept the worst of his sadness to himself. He had been snubbed by the County, who looked on him as a parvenu tradesman, which perhaps he was, though his success had done no harm to their continuing prosperity, either. Even the working men hereabouts treated him with no more than a suspect veneer of respect. He had tried to organise a shoot over his hills – what he had tried to call a park warming, and then with hollow laughter a park cooling, when the gentry had one after another pleaded polite engagements elsewhere; and even the beaters and drivers had shown water-tight, cap-fumbling reasons why they could not beat or drive on that particular day.

Esmond Fuller was on the right track when he called his daughter a Radical, though he could afford to make a pleasantry of it, since he knew he could trust her not to embarrass him. She knew, without breaking his heart by reminding him, how much he had lost. They agreed to differ, and revelled in the battles that arose from their differences. She went out to look for district visiting and good works, but found that it was all being done; her intrusion seemed as bitterly resented by the recipients as by the Establishment. She was on the side of these squalid Suffragettes – but could not answer her father's scorn at the methods they were using.

I do not think that it ever occurred to Esmond Fuller that his daughter was gradually submerging even her sincerity under her kindness and pity for him; it chafed as it dawned on her, too late to change her ways without a personal holocaust, that her kindness and pity were in any case not doing him any good.

Then Frank Lomas came to Dead-Nettle Drift. An ingenuous ex-Queen's Corporal with a copy-book sense of decency and a strong taste for Herculean work-loads; a suppressed Radical with a disgust at pretentiousness and a deep sadness at what she had already seen of the injustices of common life. It is surprising that Esmond Fuller did not see the likelihood of events earlier than he did.

Frank Lomas had accumulated a little money from somewhere – not a lot. Savings from army pay, some sort of bounty for his aggregate war service, a grant from a regimental charity for his injury; this, that and the other, all carefully husbanded; even the sale of pieces of embroidery, which he had learned in his hospital bed, to the nurses who had helped him to regain the command of his shattered leg. In all it was a modest sum – but he spent a carefully calculated share of it the morning he came away from Margreave Hall (without seeing Isobel Fuller again on the way).

He bought timber, hinges, hooks, hasps and padlocks. There were tools he would need in the Drift: gads, for wedging out faces of rock; kibbles – iron-bound buckets for hauling up ore; a bucker, a flat-headed hammer for dressing the lead; a triangular spade, a range of crow-bars. There were men in Margreave who knew what he was about and could have equipped him twenty times over from the old implements cluttering their sheds. But they clung jealously to their own. They did not offer and he did not ask. He left precise requirements with the Margreave blacksmith.

It took him three quarters of a day to swing a door over the entrance to the Drift, strictly resisting tempta-tion to be side-tracked into any experimental chipping in the mine itself. By late afternoon he had made a start on the interior of the cottage, tearing out mouldering plaster into a heap in the middle of the living-room without regard for superficial appearances.

He was amid and astride a mountain of mildew and dust when Isobel Fuller appeared in the frame of the doorway. He had not heard her horse's hooves. She held out an unsealed envelope, second-time used. Fuller often made great play over outrageous economies.

'My father has sent you your agreement – also your rent-book.'

He kicked a sliver of broken lath off his toes, wiped his hands on his corduroy trousers and took the papers from her. He looked casually into the little book, saw that the first four weeks had been entered as paid.

'My father says that it would be gross exploitation to make any charge until you are in position to start work,' she said. 'That's Papa all over. He may seem ferocious when he's negotiating a deal, but at bottom he's so generous, you'd wonder how he ever kept us out of

34

the poor-house. I don't suppose you've ever read Goldsmith's *The Man in Black*?'

'I'm afraid I haven't.'

'I don't suppose your life's given you much time for reading?'

'That has all depended on where I was. Life in the army was nine-tenths killing time. Some of us did read books – when they were about. Someone lent me *The Trumpet Major* when I was in the Base Hospital. I've read *Doctor Thorne*, quite a few by Sir Walter Scott. And *The Newcombes*, *The Book of Snobs* – '

It was unintentional, but devastating. She blushed flaming red.

'I'm sorry. I ought to have realised – '

He was slow to see the significance of her confusion.

'By William Makepeace Thackeray,' he said.

'I know.'

'Well, Miss, I must ask you to excuse me now. There's a certain stage I've set myself to reach before sunset.'

She looked round at the filth and decay. 'You really mean you're intending to live here?'

'Come back and see it in another forty-eight hours, Miss. I'll guarantee you'll not recognise it.'

'I'd like to. I'd like to look in from time to time and see how you're doing.'

'You're very welcome, Miss.'

'If I do, you'll not think I'm – spying?'

'Why should you be?'

When she had gone, he was annoyed with himself for having made no effort to detain her. To all intents and purposes he had asked her to go. He had not desisted from his work for more than a passing minute, had not even had the courtesy to see her to the threshold of his doorless door and watch her ride over the green hummocks into the more genteel reaches of the park.

There was one single image foremost in his mind: her standing, looking with incredulity verging on horror at the repellent debris under which he was almost submerged.

Two days later, almost precisely to the hour, she returned. The litter was all out of sight now, buried under the dead waste of the mine. The inside walls had been washed down, the earth floor dug over and tamped, dangerous rungs in the staircase ladder replaced by new wood. Lomas was astride the roof-ridge when he saw her approaching across country. He came down at once and was ready to receive her when she dismounted, a wood fire enlivening the hearth and a kettle on the trivet.

'You've worked wonders,' she said.

'A lesson I learned in the army. The art of roughing it is not to rough it at all, as far as it's in your own hands. Can I offer you a cup of tea?'

'I'd like nothing more.'

He made it strong and richly orange in colour. She noticed that he had brought basic house-ware, had two cups and saucers ready on a tray, fidgeted with consternation when he saw that dust had settled on the milk.

They talked; about lead and what were his hopes, and at what angles he was going to drive out his trial borings. He was conscious of some change in the passing of time, as if all that was happening now was on a different plane from everyday living. Their talk was making frightening inroads into the rest of the day's working programme. He was utterly unbothered at the knowledge.

'I'm holding you up,' she said at last. 'You were on the roof doing something. I saw you a mile off.'

'Stopping a gap or two. It's as good as done.'

'And what is the rest of the day's target?'

36

'I was hoping to make a start on the glazing.'

'May I help? I've never done it before, but I've watched men at work.'

'That's all I can say for myself. But you'll get filthy dirty.'

'I promise to wash before my next meal.'

So he delayed his return to the roof to show her how to mix the putty, though she was itching to get to work independently. Then, perched up overlooking the slag-heap of the Drift, knocking in a nail to hold the last of his slates, he could no longer see her, could only hear the occasional scratch of her scraper against the wood-work, the tap as she drove in a tack to hold a pane.

Before she left, he told her that he had to be away for the next three days. It suddenly loomed large to him that there must be no misunderstanding between them. She must not come here and find him missing, thinking him perhaps gone away for ever, so that a week or two might pass before it came to her ears that he was back again.

Yet while he was away, she did actually ride over to look at the site. And how pathetically bare and barren it looked to her now: the new, freshly creosoted wood-work sealing off the entrance tunnel to the mine, the austere and solid, impervious front door that he had fixed to the cottage; the formidable padlocks hanging from the hasps. She held her hands beside her eyes and peered through the window – the lights that she had fixed for him herself. Inside, everything looked much more spacious than she had ever imagined, and clinic-ally clean – as clean, at any rate, as untreated limestone walls and a trodden soil floor could be expected to be.

Lomas knew that she had been. She must have sat for an hour and more on the gangue – the accumulation of mineral waste of the generations of earlier strugglers

– knocking one fist-sized cobble against another to chip out the morsels of shining ore too insignificant for previous attention. She had produced enough in all to fill about three tea-cups. And she had wrapped it in a neckerchief, knotted at the corners, which she had left on a corner of his doorstep: her contribution to his dish.

Although I am writing with hindsight, not putting pen to paper until the whole story was closed, I do not find it easy to write of Isobel Fuller's developing feelings for Frank Lomas. I must not make too much of a woman's natural bent for helping out in a domestic emergency – or of her possibly disinterested admiration for an Augean project. Lomas on the other hand was frankly in love with her from the moment she had almost walked on to his clenched fist. He told me so freely; and although he recognised that there were enormous difficulties of practicability and status, he accepted the situation with typical cheerfulness.

Miss Fuller was naturally less forthcoming when I came to question her. She had had a shock which led quickly to a complete breakdown. When I talked to her, she was barely in command of herself, and there were confusing contradictions in some of what she said.

But I heard another haunting story when Frank Lomas was ultimately in confessional mood. In the early days of their acquaintance, she had found herself becoming obsessed by the thought of his wounded leg. She wanted to see him take off his repulsive boot, to look at the scarred and mangled flesh, the unnaturally twisted knots of torn and atrophied muscle. She knew she would want to avert her eyes, but she wanted to make herself stare until the sight became innocuously familiar to her. Then she brought herself to stretch out her hand and smooth her fingers over the cold wound. Lomas was afraid she would dream of it at night.

Three days after leaving Margreave, Frank returned, riding with his crippled leg outstretched over the shafts of a borrowed carrier's cart, loaded with second-hand furniture: a bed and bedding, a cupboard, a whitewood table, two kitchen chairs, two foot-stools, fire-irons, cooking pots, a wash-hand stand and a framed (and damp-stained) lithograph of Lord Roberts directing a charge against Botha at Bergendal. It was a slow, rumbling, jogging load of miscellaneous necessities and comforts which he drove along the rutted track to Dead-Nettle Drift.

He stabled the horse and worked by storm-lantern well into the night, deploying his effects about the cottage. With little more than three hours' sleep – on the first bed that he had owned in his own right ever in his life – he was away at dawn to return the cart to the carrier, returning on foot about midday. He worked all the afternoon, clearing rubbish from the mouth of the mine, but looking often over his shoulder so as not to miss a full view of Isobel when she rode up through the pasture behind the cottage. And she did just that, at what he was already beginning to think of as her usual time.

He at once went in to make tea, the kettle already filled and waiting only to be pushed back on the hob. He could not wait to show her round his home. She laughed at his boyish sense of urgency.

'But it's lovely.'

There were a chair and stool on either side of the hearth. She forbore to comment on it.

'Did you find – ?'

'Your lead chippings? Yes. Every little helps.'

He did not tell her that he would not be using them.

He had decided that to use gangue chippings to help fill the dish would have been cheating the Bar Master.

'I felt as if I was really getting you going,' she said. 'I got lead from the mine before you did.'

She looked up at the appalling lithograph, and said nothing.

'I've got a few bits and pieces that I'll bring over. We've some old rush matting that'll come to no harm on this floor.'

'One day I shall pave it with bricks. Or pammets. That can wait. First things first, I always say.'

'And you need a cloth for the table. Curtains. I've got one or two things that I'd collected to give to the cottagers, only they didn't seem to want them.'

'I'll tell you what,' he said. 'Why don't you come and have supper with me? Next week. Tuesday. There'll be something to celebrate on Tuesday. That's when I aim to have filled my dish.'

'I don't know what on earth my father would say.'

'Bring him with you.'

Scintillant laughter. When she had gone, he was uncertain whether she had agreed to come or not. He looked for her on the days in between, at what he now thought of as tea-time, but she did not come. He went into the town to stock up with provisions, had a mutton stew simmering in his pot. The thought began to needle him that he might be building for himself a monumental illusion.

She did come. Without her father. But they were not alone together for long.

Leitmotif: unforeseen callers.

CHAPTER FIVE

'Of course,' she said, 'you're no stranger to mines.'

'To lead-mines I am.'

And he told her of his boyhood near the Nottingham-shire border: how he had left school from Standard Five to follow his elder brothers down the pit. He described the back-to-back terraces curling over the slag valleys. He spoke of the long months, from mid-autumn to mid-spring, when he had never seen daylight from Monday to Saturday: the jungle-beat of clog-irons down-hill through cruel morning frosts, the afternoon shift dispersing through the shunting wagons at the pit-head, the last gesture of day a bloody wound in the shale-coloured skies behind the winding-gear (she thought again of his ruined leg).

As a boy he had been gullible, the butt of every practical joker on the playground, street and shift. He knew it himself now, could laugh about it with re-hearsed, detached wisdom. But there were some things, she knew, that he would never tell her, admissions that he still had not made, even to himself.

On his first day at the face some irresponsible buffoon had sent him along a forgotten gallery on the sort of tom-fool errand with which impressionable apprentices are tormented in every walk of life. *Go to the store-shed on H Gallery, ask for Tom Tweed. Ask him for a straight S-hook for Billy Haigh's team. Make sure you sign for it.* Within minutes he was lost, turning back in panic, certain that it was here he had turned left and there right. He only half understood his Davey lamp, was certain it was showing a concentration of gas. In the distance a leak in a drainage channel sounded like a waterfall. He came into a tunnel that looked better used – fresh propped and vetted, metal rails shining with a high polish. Then thunder, an onslaught of murderous wheels. *Get back where you should be, you bloody young fool*: a train of six wagons hurtling past him with inches to spare, white eyes in a black face under a veteran's helmet cursing him to perdition.

His father rapidly became ashamed to have him in the same pit, his mother even more distraught as she saw all hopes recede that he might ever grow into a man. His uncles, his cousins, the demagogues of the union, they all cursed the owners, the fire-damp, the after-damp, blue scars on their foreheads, the dust in their lungs. Yet they clung to the rock-face, in love with their own martyrdom. *Grow up and show you are a man.* Men never turned their backs on trouble.

On Sundays there was daylight, even sunshine, slanting down through the dust from the chapel windows. Chapel on Sunday mornings, Young Men's Bible Class on Sunday afternoons, Chapel again in the evening. Chapel taught you that dissatisfaction with your lot was a sin.

> *This grace has been purchased at infinite cost,*
> *And all who reject it must die.*

(Lomas had gone to Chapel in the Market Square on his first Sunday evening in Margreave, and had not missed a Sunday evening since. He wore a black suit in the style of the 1880s that he had preserved somewhere amongst his belongings, and stood with his hair fiercely brushed, drowning all his neighbours in his toneless tenor. Chapel was against strong drink. It was the only respect in which he was a back-slider – except on Sundays. He never went into the *Adventurers' Arms* on Sundays.)

'No wonder you went into the army,' Isobel Fuller said.

In advance, she had decided to be gracious about the mutton stew. It tickled her to think what her father might have said, if he could have seen her at the table in front of such a bowlful. It was high amongst his illusions that he had risen to refined gastronomic standards. But Frank Lomas's stew turned out to be one of the tastiest dishes she had ever eaten. She happily accepted a second helping.

'It wasn't as easy as that,' Lomas told her. 'The army was no sacred cow in our valley and street. It was coal that made men of us, not charging the *kopjes*. I did have a letter from my father at last, while I was waiting for overseas draft, somewhere along the south coast – months after I'd given up hope of ever hearing from him again. He wished me well – but I'd hurt him and disappointed him. He didn't say so in so many words, but he'd credited me with more common sense than to enlist for a soldier. And I know he thought that I was running away, turning my back on my difficulties instead of seeing them through. I'd never be able to hold up my face amongst miners again. And suppose that the troops were called in for strike-breaking?'

Isobel Fuller looked at him for a moment with such penetration that he turned his eyes away.

'So that's why you've come back to mining,' she said.

'It isn't the same.'

'It would serve your purpose, if you could make your living from it, wouldn't it?'

'I hope I shall chip out enough for my daily bread.'

'So why choose Dead-Nettle Drift? It's common talk that there are twenty or thirty mines within a two-mile radius of here where there are seams enough still for a life-time of hacking. They only want outlay on drainage

– plus staying-power, which you have in abundance. But there's nothing in Dead-Nettle. Even I can see that.'

'I think I shall be proving you wrong.'

'You think you have what they call inside information?'

Lomas signified that he had – and had no reason to doubt it. But his usual prattling candour seemed to dry up. He was not going to tell her about it.

'From whom?' she asked bluntly, trying to maintain the inconsequence of table-talk.

'From a man I can trust.'

I think that Isobel first felt the pangs of a kind of jealousy in that moment. There was a wing shuttered off in his life that he did not want to open up to her. Perhaps she might have gone on to force his hand.

But at that juncture there were horses arriving with ebullient noise on the rubble outside, the extroversion of men of high spirit challenging the world at large; men for whom the peace and privacy of the people about them were something that had to be punctured.

'It looks as if old Frank's got the place stockaded up for a siege.'

'Come on, Frank, open up, let's be having you, on parade, show a leg, show us one of them, anyway. By God, I do believe he's got a woman in there.'

Frank Lomas had drunk two pints of beer in the *Adventurers' Arms* most week-nights since his arrival in Margreave, and there had been some subtle change in the attitude of the regulars to him. But there was no open hand of friendship. No man would have shown pleasure to see him come in, but he was treated less now as if he were some hidden menace. They thought of him mostly as a harmless kind of fool. He had faced a similar attitude in the coal-pit as an adolescent; again as a recruit on the parade-ground. But these men in the pub played no practical jokes on him. They were too set in their ways, too staid, almost too dull in spirit for that. There was no youth left in them – and besides that, to have pulled his leg would have been too far along the road to admitting him to equality.

He was simply the man without gumption, the man with no notion about what he was doing: who didn't know how to hang a door over an adit (though in fact his carpentry was as good as any of theirs). He had spent a small fortune that he was never going to retrieve, he had ordered the wrong tools from the blacksmith, he was preparing to winter in quarters that were surely going to tumble about his ears. They were prepared to believe no good of him, and had settled down to wait for a gratifying catastrophe.

But he was beginning to make some sort of progress with them. The night he entertained Isobel Fuller to a mutton stew, he was actually missed in the *Adventurers' Arms*.

'Where's the old hand, then?'

'Fallen down one of his ten-inch shafts.'

'Gone to Derby to settle with the Railway Board. They're running a heavy goods branch-line, out from Wirksworth up to Dead-Nettle.'

But a few minutes later the *Adventurers' Arms* received a visit that was to unsettle the local peace for some weeks to come.

Two men came in, one of them obviously the shadow and tool of the other – men aged on the thirty mark, hearty complexions and bodies in the full flush of fresh air and vigorous living. They seemed to have travelled some distance, for their clothes, though not of working cut, bore a certain weariness of the cloth, the nap worn, and with a bagginess at the knees that belied their evident concern about their appearance. There was dust encrusted in the welts of boots whose fastidious polish was normally buffed up with a soft cloth several times a day. The more forward of the two had slickly pomaded hair and a moustache with waxed tips that proclaimed him a military man – or was intended to give that impression. Both were wearing black satin ties, the leader's tied in a faultless Windsor knot, his friend's in an Academy bow.

The effect of their entry on the men in the *Adventurers'* was complex. It was less of a corporate reaction than the one which had first greeted Frank Lomas – as if they had known within themselves that he was not a man to be feared, merely to be mocked, whereas there were unknown possibilities in these two that demanded circumspection.

The man with the military air asked for rooms for the night – but without that touch of polite humility that might have increased his chances in a strange community. There was a threat of irritability about him, as one accustomed to having servants at his beck and call : an ill-judged approach in the *Adventurers' Arms*. I do not know whether two bedrooms might have been available for single men. This man destroyed by the curl of his lip their chances of getting them if they were. They were offered a shared bed, and saw that they had to accept it or move on.

'Ay, well, it'll be better than Spytfontein.'

'Aye – or Reddersburg.'

Some of the men in the inn were quicker than others at putting a name to the principal visitor's face, but one who had no difficulty, even from the first, was Tiggy Slack. The little grocer, in his own semi-circle of cronies, seemed to take a half step back into the shadows as the couple came in round the outside door, and he crept out behind them while they were still negotiating with the landlord. The man with the moustache, however, wheeled round suddenly and insolently watched him go, as if enjoying the satisfaction of something he had expected.

They knew now: Gilbert Slack – but there was no move to acknowledge him. Most assemblies of men include one sycophant who will weaken a common front, but no one played out of turn here.

Conversation became subdued on both sides, Slack and his companion muttering over their plans for looking over the neighbourhood. The others returned before long to the well worn idiocies of Frank Lomas.

'How long do we give him, then – another month? Then he'll be sitting in the Market Place with his cap on the pavement and a row of chalk pictures on the slabs.'

'He's been to the Hall. Maybe he's talked the old man into chucking some funds down the Drift.'

'And would the old man do that without having the place surveyed?'

They had supreme confidence that nothing could happen in Margreave without their knowledge.

'Fuller didn't make his kind of money by adventuring in places like Dead-Nettle.' (The *Adventurers' Arms* is named, not after romantic swashbucklers, but after bygone investors in mineral working.)

'Dead-Nettle?'

Gilbert Slack did not appear to have been listening, but he swung round at the mention of the mine. The previous speaker took a breath, as if making up his mind whether to answer or not.

'Did you say Dead-Nettle?'

'An old stope on the north-east flank of Whim Hill.'

'I know damned well where Dead-Nettle is.' There was

something in his voice that was not accustomed to being played with.

'I should think you do.'

'Who's working Dead-Nettle, then?'

'Nobody you'd know.'

'A comer-in? Not a Margreave man?'

'Nobody knows where he's from. He could even be one of your lot.'

'Our lot?'

'Nay, Edward,' someone else said. 'The old hand's never been a soldier – not with a foot like that.'

'What about his foot?'

'He wears a big boot – moves his leg all in one piece.'

And thereupon Gilbert Slack laughed – an unhealthy, bottled-up guffaw, that he seemed nevertheless to be having to force out of himself. He nudged his friend with his elbow, and he too started to laugh.

'Old Peg-leg Lomas.'

There was something about their laughter that did not seem genuine.

'Old Peg-leg Lomas, trying to get rich on a Margreave stope? Where is he living, then? Likely to be in here tonight, is he?'

'He's living on the quarter. He's done up the cottage.'

'After a fashion.'

'How long's he been working it? Making a go of it, is he?'

Slack really wanted to know, but was trying not to let them see just how urgently. It was remarkable what insight and memory some of these Margreave onlookers had, when I finally persuaded them to talk to me.

'He's been here a week or two. He hasn't freed the meer yet. Been roofing and dooring.'

'And sucking around Esmond Fuller.'

'Who's Esmond Fuller?'

'The new man who's bought Margreave Hall.'

Gilbert Slack finished his beer. 'Harry, this is too good to put off until tomorrow. We'll carry our stuff upstairs and then take a gentle canter round to Dead-Nettle.'

The man who later described this scene to me said that if Slack had ordered Harry to come without finishing his drink, he was sure he would have obeyed without question.

Frank Lomas and Isobel heard the hooves and voices outside on the rubble, and for a moment Lomas sat stiff-backed as if trying to wish away the interruption. But then there was hammering on the new wooden door, so imperative that it could no longer be ignored. He got up and lifted the latch.

'Gilbert! Harry!'

'Peg-leg! Who'd have thought the three of us would ever have got here?'

Gusty handshakes and back-slapping; Frank Lomas was now all vacuous broad smiles.

'To tell you the truth, Frank, I'd half a mind to bring my own dish to Dead-Nettle. But you've pipped me to it. And if there's anyone I'd rather have seen get here before me, it's you. Don't I get an introduction?'

He faced Isobel Fuller as if he had made more progress with her in ten seconds than Frank had in ten days. Her response to this whirlwind arrival was a mixture of plain disappointment and positive resentment. It was the end of her tête-à-tête with this slowly self-revealing man. She would not have gone so far as to admit that she felt as if these men were robbing her of Frank. But they belonged to a slice of his past of which she knew nothing and which, every instinct told her, had been less than worthy of him. And it was not merely that they were reminding him of it. They would drag him back to it if they could. They would revive in him some pride in the wildness of the years they had in common; if they had not happened along, he would never have looked back over his shoulder.

She at once conceived a dislike of Gilbert Slack that was increased by every inflexion of his voice and every theatrical sweep of his hands. They were badly kept hands; Slack was clearly a man sickeningly vain of his appearance, but he overlooked his hands. And she knew in those first few seconds that he would do his best to rob her of Frank Lomas, for some purpose of his own – perhaps because he was one of those men who saw no greater challenge than another man's integrity. And as for the other one, he was a mere loiterer at Slack's elbow, as faithful as some yellow mongrel who refuses to be put off by a kick and an empty dish.

'No, please don't get up.'

But she rose, and Slack gripped her fingers in an over-warm hand which maintained its grasp longer than it need have done. He looked as if he wholly misinterpreted her purpose in being alone here with Frank; as if he imputed to her, in all naturalness, the most squalid of motives – moreover as if he himself were more than half sharing her enjoyment of them. In fact, he looked at her as if he were experimenting with her in his own mind; as if, too, he knew that she was under no illusion about his thoughts. Then his eyes wandered casually over to Frank, as if to indicate that he was quite content to leave her to him; it was only fair – for the time being, at any rate. And Isobel Fuller found everything about Gilbert Slack revolting – the glistening grease on his hair, the sweating pores in his skin, above all his un-questioning confidence that no one would ever repulse him. He must have been repulsed on countless occasions, she reflected, but he was the sort of man to shrug it off as if he had barely noticed.

'It might just run to a couple more bowls of stew,' Lomas said.

The man called Harry accepted his as a man who eats what happens to be going. Slack took a couple of mouthfuls and then seemed to forget about it. Frank had lent him an old spoon, worn out of shape along its outside edge, with his army number stamped on the handle. Slack looked at it satirically.

'Well, Corporal Lomas, it seems a long time now since that night on the *Karroo*.'

'Yes. I shall never forget that moon.'

'That bloody moon – I beg your pardon, Miss Fuller – we'd said that before, but this time we meant it. That was the night I told you about this place, Frank.'

'That's why I'm here,' Lomas said, with painful sentimentality.

'What a memory!'

'I think I can remember every word you said, Gilbert – and you weren't wrong in any detail that mattered.'

'Well, you've beaten me to it, Frank. If you hadn't got here first, I'd have been here prospecting. You'd better watch out that I don't have the Bar Master nicking your stowe.'[1]

'I don't think you'd ever do that, Gilbert.'

'So how are you going to tackle it, Frank? You'll carry on driving the way the Drift runs?'

'No. I see no future in that. The Old Man[2] stopped where he did because he knew he was wasting his time.'

---

[1] A traditional ceremony by which a miner may claim another man's neglected working.

[2] The Old Man: a generic term in regional lore, referring to the previous miner and all his antecedents; also, confusingly, it is sometimes used to mean the waste he left behind.

'That's what I've always thought.'

'So I shall drive trials in other places: up left, down left, up right, down right, in on the slant, down on the plumb.'

'My plan exactly. You don't want a partner, do you?'

Isobel Fuller could have answered that for him. But even Frank Lomas showed his unease at the suggestion.

'That would be two men's eggs in one basket, Gilbert. There are other mines about, if you've got a fancy for one. Some of them might be a sight more profitable than Dead-Nettle. Why not take one of those? We might form a co-operative later, when we've something to smelt.'

Gilbert Slack laughed.

'Not for me, brother. I'm no miner. Too much like work for yours truly. I've always had a feeling about Dead-Nettle – but you're here and it's yours. I as good as gave it to you, that night we talked about it. I'd never go back on that offer. You *had* just saved my life.'

Why? Isobel found herself wondering.

'So how are you going to dig your tunnels, Frank?'

He pushed the remainder of his stew in the direction of Harry, who applied himself to it as if he had not noticed that it was a different bowl.

'Gads,' Lomas said. 'I'm having them made, for wedging out the mother-rock. Fire-setting, maybe, to crack the walls. Quick-lime, perhaps.'

'Not dynamite? Dynamite's the thing nowadays.'

'I've heard enough shot-firing for one life-time – above ground and under.'

'I know where I can get some for you. It would save you weeks of grafting.'

But Frank had clearly taken against high explosive.

'I'd rather do it my way. I may not get rich fast, but I mean to enjoy myself.'

'Well – if you ever change your mind – '

Shortly after that, Isobel Fuller announced that she ought to be going home. And here lay a problem to which Frank had found only a tentative solution, since she had a horse and he had none. He had assumed that he would walk with her on the leading rein until they were at least within sight of the Hall. It was Gilbert Slack who said that of course it would be no trouble for him and Harry to escort the young lady. Lomas suggested that he should accompany them on foot.

'Then that's three of us tied to a walking pace,' Gilbert said. 'And Harry and I are more than ready for our beds. We've been on the road all day. What's the matter, Frank old son, don't you trust us? There's safety in numbers, when all's said and done.'

Isobel Fuller was at least as uneasy about the arrangement as Lomas was, but she felt as if her wits had deserted her, and saw no way out of the trap. There was no way, just no way at all, of disappearing from the sight of those two men. She could hardly change her mind now and say that she wanted to spend another hour with Frank; that would be a gift to Slack's unpleasant mind. She thought of pretending that her horse was lame, which would give Frank the chance to come at his own speed; but Slack would see through the prevarication. She was a young woman who took pride in having thrown off the shackles of convention – at least, in outlook. Did it matter so much to her what Slack thought or might not think? Could she hate a man so much, after so short a time in his company?

And there *was* safety in numbers; she had a horse well trained to her will which might also, in certain circumstances, be used as a weapon of defence.

Lomas, of course, trusted his friends implicitly, but he was not a happy man as he watched the trio ride away from the cottage. Six pairs of hooves crunched into the gravelly gangue, and so dark was the night that within seconds his visitors merged into it.

CHAPTER SIX

Lomas slept badly. There were problems on his mind to which he kept finding decisive solutions, only to come up against the sickeningly familiar snags as his brain swung in overlapping circles.

He wished Gilbert Slack six thousand miles from here, back in South Africa, up-river trading in South America, gold-panning in frozen Canada. They had talked of all these things, believing themselves and each other for hours on end in the idle watches of the Transvaal nights. Yet there had been nothing insincere in Lomas's welcome of the pair last night. They had been army friends, and Lomas, though I am inclined rather easily to call him simple-minded, was no simpleton; he knew what an army friend meant and what it did not mean. There could be absolute trust in bad spots, absolute honesty in the illuminating scepticism of platoon life, absolute loyalty in the face of the enemy, whether that meant Boer settlers or one's own officers. There could be a united front against civilian populations that deserved no more than to be exploited. There had been almost passionate exchanges of confidence in the long hours of boredom, long distances from the sources of one's heartbreaks. One listened for an hour and bought the right to talk in one's turn. One gave assurances of blood-brother understanding – but later, both parties forgot. Especially Gilbert Slack; would Gilbert Slack clutter his brain for five minutes with someone else's woes, unless these could possibly be turned to his own advantage?

On the other hand, would Gilbert Slack ever forget, in all its trivial telling detail, any ancient tale or rumour that might be docketed for his future use?

Lomas knew Slack as what was sometimes called an honest rogue – a cheat and rapscallion who attracted men by his very effrontery, whose iniquities were usually on such a small scale that his victims suffered little more than irritant damage. He was open-handed when it came to sharing out his quick profits. And he was a consummate raconteur of his own misdeeds.

Gilbert Slack had had a good deal to do with Lomas's being in the army at all. He had been the object of picaresque envy to the colourless lad from the pit-bottom who had suddenly heard drums, seen red coats and grasped that tropical moons were not beyond his own reach. And, in all fairness, Slack had not abandoned young Lomas when they were in the ranks together. Himself a trained soldier, he had kept the recruit out of at least some of the trouble that he might have been in. He had encouraged Lomas to keep company with him – for Slack liked an impressionable following, just as he was now wandering the kingdom to the silent adulation of Harry Burgess. Though, by God, Lomas hoped that there was more to himself than there was to Harry.

Once, before going abroad, when they were under canvas on the Isle of Thanet, they indulged in a week-end's wandering after a field-day in the Kentish marshes. On an afternoon of golden spring they had come into

St Nicholas-at-Wade where, with a wink, Slack had taken him into the village store. There Gilbert had pleaded desperate thirst, and while the blousy shop-keeper went into the back quarters to fetch them glasses of water, he filled the pockets of his tunic with apples and potted meat, sardines and night-lights for midnight card-schools. Seeing Lomas's unease as they put distance between themselves and the shop, he had rammed hard at the still active non-conformist conscience. 'Not worried about that old bitch, are you? She'll still be shovelling money into her till while you and I are wiping the blood out of our eyes with the backs of our hands.' Slack often claimed to be redressing social un-fairness. The world owed him a living, and he got what he could from those of its inhabitants who were slow enough to fall for his wiles. But he never put himself at any great risk. When Lomas took stock of the years, it was remarkable how rarely Slack had been even on the fringes of real trouble.

Now Lomas was jealous of him : that was the kernel of the sleepless night. Blinded himself by Isobel Fuller, he had to believe that Gilbert Slack would be similarly overwhelmed. And so keen were his memories of Slack's facetious charms that he could imagine Isobel being taken in despite her finer judgement. Slack's glib tongue would not have been idle during that dark ride home.

It was not that Lomas feared that Slack might attempt anything untoward on the way. Slack had had adven-tures with women, but it was never his way to take unconventional risks. The nearest that Lomas had ever heard him boast of sexual criminality was a ruse by which he had done a garrison prostitute out of her fee.

He knew that Isobel was safe from actual assault. But he also knew that if Slack wanted to clear the decks for himself, there was one story that he could let slip with devastating finality. Lomas felt clammy and cold on his second-hand mattress at the thought of it. It wouldn't stop short at a breakage with Isobel Fuller.

Then he tried to comfort himself with the thought that Gilbert Slack would surely not stay long in Margreave. Hard labour for minimal returns had never appealed to Slack's temperament. There was no one here who wanted him. His own father had thrown him out and disowned him. Lomas recognised now that the message he had carried to the grocer's shop had been sent as a gesture of impudence. Even if you gave Slack the freedom of a mine with seams a yard thick glistening out of the wall at eye-level, neither the labour nor the hours would have appealed to him for long.

Unless, of course –

Unless Slack indeed saw the possibilities of Isobel Fuller, in which case he was capable of accepting temporary discomfort in the interests of a waiting game. And if that were Slack's ploy, then one well-timed jibe would be enough to under-swipe Lomas's chances. One of the gaps in Lomas's conceptions was his inability to credit Isobel Fuller with any judgement of men whatsoever.

He gave up before dawn any further effort to sleep, came down his ladder and collected his tools. It was physical work that he needed. Normally a man of inflexible patterns, his one thought this morning was to get out and be tearing with his hands at the rock-face. On any other morning, his first thoughts would have been to breakfast and wash up his three or four crocks, to rake out yesterday's fire and lay the grate for a touch of a match this evening. In twenty minutes' fettling he would have his home as orderly as a barrack-room before First Parade.

Not this morning. He snatched himself a hunk of

bread and cheese, made no drink because he had no fire, satisfied himself with a glass of milk, lit his hurricane lamp and unlocked the door to the adit.

There was comfort in the familiarity of the underground air, the damp intermingled smells of lime and clay, the primeval walls that indefinitely belonged to him. He went to a patch that he had already singled out for early attention – a spot where behind the semi-translucent calcite face there was a darker stain that might possibly be a pocket of ore. He hammered in the edge of a wedge and began to score out his area of action.

He worked more clumsily than usual – I think there must have been something of the petrified personality of Gilbert Slack in his target patch – and once his gad slipped and gashed the back of his hand. It was one of those injuries where the sight of blood some minutes later was his first knowledge that he had hurt himself. He paused to suck his knuckles, then worked on.

Half an hour later he had exposed the black shadow and saw indeed that it was a knot of pure ore, and a few minutes later succeeded in breaking some of it out, not stopping now to pick up the bits that were scattered on the mine floor. Already he had within hand's reach as much as he could have gathered in half a day of chipping amongst the gangue; now was not the time to worry over splinters. Another quarter of an hour and he had the whole lump out – a piece about the combined size of his two fists. It would cover a useful corner of the dish.

But after that – nothing. It was a single isolated blob of sulphide, thrown up in the solidifying fountain as the crusts of the earth were cooling. There was no more lead in evidence, behind or beside it. He collected together what he had gained and set to work levering out more of the parent rock near the same spot. For two hours he worked with no more result than a heap of worthless spar.

At mid-morning he came out for a breather, went over to the house and found himself more bread and cheese, was disgusted at the disorder in which he had left things. He escaped by turning his back on it and returning to the Drift. Having started in one particular spot, he would work that out to its logical conclusions and then make one of his test borings.

He worked for the rest of the day, ignoring hunger, not needing rest, hurling physical energy against stone, impelled always by the thought that one more blow might uncover a small fortune. I have already implied that he was almost a pathological optimist: in no way did this show itself more typically than in his onslaught against a daunting, to other men clearly futile, task. He worked with fury, no less, his hopes undulled by the vistas of valueless rock that he exposed. Sometimes he stopped to clear aside rubble that might have been hiding a find. Once his wedge loosened a whole block of stone that split away along the line of a natural fault. He thrust in his finger-ends and broke away a massive boulder in an outburst of sheer physical ecstasy : Lomas versus bed-rock.

After that, he decided that his present scene of operation was going to yield no results, transferred his attention to the opposite wall and began to make inroads there.

But never anything. It was not for weeks, indeed months, that Lomas ultimately abandoned his efforts in Dead-Nettle; but I think that it was on this day that the possibility first realistically occurred to him that the mine might be as sterile as most men said, that he might have to think again about his whole future, might even have to limp back to the coal-field of his boyhood, begging for any employment that they could find him.

In the middle of the afternoon he broke the shank of what was by now his favourite wedge and came out to fetch a replacement. He stood for a moment by the door of the Drift and took stock of the grey, pulverised waste. A horse-fly hovered over a sorry clump of rag-wort.

Something was out of place in the scene before him, and although it should have been obvious, he did not at first see what it was: smoke rising from the cottage chimney. The front door was closed, but as he walked across the gangue, he saw someone moving about behind the window. He quickened his steps, recognised Isobel Fuller in the act of setting his broom back in its corner. The fire had been lit, the derangement from last evening's supper-party had been tidied up, a length of old but respectable wool-clipping rug had been laid across the hearth.

'I came to say thank you for last night. And on the spur of the moment, I thought I'd give you a little surprise. Better than just leaving a card, don't you think?'

She was wearing clothes in which he had not seen her before: jodhpurs and a three-quarter coat. He had previously only seen her ride in long skirts.

'You got home all right last night, then?'

A stupid question: but it was so near to the surface of his mind that he had to ask it.

'Do you know of any reason why I shouldn't have?'

It was no more than a pleasantry, but there was a playful mockery in her tone that abashed him a good deal more than it need have done. She hastened to follow it up.

'And while we're on the subject, or something akin to it, may I say something?'

'Anything you like.'

'I don't like your friends.'

That was a relief, but after the way in which he had received them, there was no logic in trying to disclaim their friendship.

'Especially not Colour-Sergeant Slack.'

'He was not a Colour-Sergeant. He was a private soldier.'

'I'll believe you. He told me he was a Colour-Sergeant.'

'He didn't try – ?'

She smiled at his coyness.

'No. As you so neatly put it, he didn't try. If he had, he would have been up against a prancing steed, as well as a riding-crop. Did you expect that he would – *try*?'

'I'm sure it would never have occurred to him.'

'Frank, you are pricelessly sweet. That, at least, might have been expressed with more gallantry. But I must talk to you about him. I'm afraid he's going to prove something of a nuisance. Shall I make a pot of tea?'

'Yes, please do. How: a nuisance? I don't think he'll stay here long.'

'He will. He has ingratiated himself with my father.'

She busied herself with the kettle.

'I came over to have supper with you last night, Frank, because I wanted to, because I usually do the things that I want to, and because there was no harm in it. I hope you'll invite me again. But you'll understand that amongst the people whom I have to spend most of my time with, it would raise a few eye-brows. I didn't tell my father I was coming, not because it gave me any pleasure to deceive him. In fact, I didn't deceive him. I simply didn't undeceive him. There'd been some talk of a missionary lantern lecture in the parish hall, and he thought I'd gone there. It saved him unnecessary worry. But Master Slack and his Sancho Panza insisted on coming right up to the Hall with me. They aren't exactly fairy horsemen with elfin feet, and Father came to the door before they could ride away. The story was that they had provided a gallant escort for me through the inspissated darkness, for which they were asked in and offered a toddy. I made a bad mistake. I took Private Slack to one side in the corridor and breathed quickly in his ear what story he had to tell.'

Probably superfluous, Lomas thought. Slack would not have been slow to spot that he had happened on some sort of deception. He would have trodden warily until he had seen where his own advantage lay.

'He is quick on the uptake, is your friend. He now thinks, of course, that he has some sort of hold over me. And so, up to a point, he has. But only up to a point. Five minutes' confessional with my father, and I can put everything right – but I'd rather not. I'd rather not have the fag of it, and I'd rather save him from days of fretting. So I sat by and listened while they talked him into giving them a job for the winter. Father was impressed by Private Slack – especially the Colour-Sergeant part – and by some of the battlefield tales that he told. So now Messrs Slack and Burgess have been engaged for estate work, finishing off all the jobs that my father has started all over the place.'

Frank Lomas was a fair man to a fault. He felt he simply must avoid possible injustice to Gilbert.

'Of course, I was invalided out, you know, and Gilbert still had his time to serve. He can't have been out very long as it is. I don't know all that's gone on in the regiment since I was discharged. He *might* have been promoted.'

'Don't be silly, Frank. You know he never would have been. He was Private Slack. And you were a corporal.'

'Queen's Corporal. Promoted in the field. By General Sir Redvers Buller in person.'

'I know. Private Slack told us all about that.'

And Lomas could suddenly find nothing at all to say. He knew beyond any shadow of doubt what version of that tale Slack would have told : the true one.

'And that's not the only thing,' Isobel said. 'He takes too much interest in Dead-Nettle Drift for my liking. He brings it back into the conversation every few minutes. Just as he did while he was here. He wants to know just how you're working and where you're going to bore next. And it isn't the lead that concerns him. He knows nothing about mining, or processing, or market value. And it was he who put you on to this mine.'

'It was. But – '

'I'm sure you had every reason to believe him at the time. I'm sure you believe him still. I can only hope for your sake that you're right and I'm wrong. The last thing I would ever want to do would be to come between you and a friend. But there is one thing that you must see. I have to break that man away from my father. I have to get him off our estate. I know he's a villain, and he hasn't come back to this village by accident. Just what he's up to, I have no idea. The fact remains, I'm not going to have him impose on my father. Nor am I prepared to have him leering at me from every corner of every terrace round the place. That's what I've come here now to tell you – because I know you have always counted him a friend.'

Frank Lomas said it then, at last. 'He's no friend of mine.'

'I'm glad to hear it. And I'm sorry to say that I think

that Dead-Nettle Drift is the least friendly gift he could ever have laid in your way.'

'That's still to be determined.'

'As you please. I would give anything to be wrong about it. But you'll not hold it against me if I see that Slack is sent packing?'

'If there's anything I can do to help –'

But Lomas knew what havoc Slack could work before he went. Slack had only to choose his moment to destroy him. He had been a fool to think there would ever be any lasting escape from Hetty Wilson. But for Slack he would never have met her in the first place.

CHAPTER SEVEN

Winter staked its claim in the advancing autumn. In the second part of November there was a sudden week of ruthless frost. Lomas drove himself hard. He was at work in the Drift before sunrise. But a changed rhythm settled into his working habits. As trial after trial brought him no new sight of ore, his first wild flurry devolved into a steady, methodical progress along the channels that he had mapped out for himself. He began to pay almost superstitious attention to the tidiness with which he cleared up his debris behind him, building little stacks and walls of gangue. It must have cost him hours that could have driven him yards deeper into the hill-side. It was not that he had yet given up all hope; but I think he was beginning consciously to put off the day when he would finally have to do so. In the meanwhile he was deriving some deep personal **reward** from the labour itself.

At first Isobel Fuller came at odd times of day, two or three times a week, according to the variations of her daily ride. On two days in succession she came in the late afternoon, and after that every day at the same time. Frank Lomas would come out of the mine, strip down to the waist whatever the weather and wash himself in a bucket in the open air before entering the cottage. By that time she had his kettle on the boil, a meal set for two on a linen cloth discarded from home that she had brought for his whitewood table. Often she brought dishes of food, and it would be a fiction to pretend that they were left-overs: sherry trifle, a cold apple-pie, a generous end of cold rib of beef. She did this, that and the other about the cottage, though Lomas could hardly be said to be in need of such service. His own housekeeping, if bleak, was never skimped of hygiene or symmetry: he might have been living in hourly expectation of a commanding officer's inspection. Isobel brought here and there a woman's touch – to which he never referred. She might have thought that he did not notice – but I believe that he did: it would simply have embarrassed him to have acknowledged his own inability to think of the things that would have pleased a lady. She once brought a couple of old gilt-painted picture-frames and asked him whether he had not any photographs from his past that he would like to put up. He then brought out an old oil-skin wallet, clearly something that had been through the war with him; but then he started extemporising with enforced gaiety about unrelated subjects. He was careful to avoid opening it in her presence. The next day the frames were on the wall; showing off a pair of studio groups, solemn massive family gatherings, apparently taken on the occasion of a mid-Victorian funeral. She never pried amongst his belongings for that wallet.

Once, in the middle of a morning, he heard her arrive – or thought he did : irregular movements on the loose stones outside, as he was lying on one shoulder, hacking away at an overhang. He laid down his tool – she made a tacit point of never interrupting him during working hours; but he was secretly glad of the break. He blew out his lamp and came to the surface, to find not Isobel Fuller waiting for him on the slag, but a little old woman in widow's weeds of a pattern that had gone out of vogue fifty years ago, though there was a certain new-ness about her costume, as if it had been long stored and little worn.

Lomas knew at once who she was : Florence Belfield, a character well known in Margreave and the *Adventurers' Arms*. Not to delve too subtly into diagnosis, she was mad : mad with a fixity that amused no one and was the frequent source of trouble for her neighbours. Accounts of her eccentricities were told factually, neither as something comic, nor as anything that deserved sympathy. Florence Belfield was a feature of the Margreave hills, as gaunt and hard-lined as the slag-heaps and the abandoned crushing-wheels. Lomas prepared himself for trouble at the sight of her. Florence Belfield took her delusions seriously and treated her enemies, which she imagined most men to be, extremely uncouthly. Isaac Grundy, Bar Master, knew her well. She had a formidable knowledge of mining case-law, and two or three times a year could be depended on to emerge from her seclusion to demand action against villains who were now mostly dead.

But there seemed nothing potentially aggressive about the withered creature who stood watching Lomas from his plateau of Dead-Nettle toad-stone. If she had been

66

to her clothing-chest to dress to impress him, then he knew intuitively that for the moment he had the upper hand, even over her hallucinations.

'So you're the young man who's working to free the Drift?'

'I am. Frank Lomas, ma'am.'

'Mrs John William Belfield – in need of your help.'

He knew from the stories that these could be fatal words. He tried to be non-committal.

It was nearly sixty years ago, as a young matron in her twenties, that Florence Belfield had been widowed by a roof-fall. In Badger's Swallet it had happened, one of the last mines in the neighbourhood ever to be profitably worked. Old Edward Fothergill, Bar Master of the day, had transferred the holding to her name in the big register. She had half a dozen miners on her pay-roll and had gone on for a year or so, working out a tapering seam. Then there had been strife underground. She had found that she was being pettily and systematically robbed, put in a spy among her workmen, which led to a fight at the working face. A man was crippled for life and his brother filled a dish in an adjacent working with the barely concealed intention of driving in a heading to poach on her diminishing reserves. She watched, spied, questioned, reported her suspicions to the Moot; much was known but nothing proven and the conflict remained unresolved, the parties embittered. Florence Belfield began to bribe the ganger who had previously cheated her, and within a few months was obsessed in the tactical direction of an underground war. There were rumours and counter-rumours, a race from the two mines towards a reputed pocket that did not in fact exist. One side or the other, no one knew which, broke through into a subterranean water-course and two men were drowned. Florence Belfield was deserted by her own men. She made an effort to carry on in Badger's single-handed, was brought out half dead when a thunder-storm over the hill brought the water in her gallery above shoulder level.

Since then she had plunged into every kind of litigation that the usages of the liberty had ever envisaged. To old Isaac Grundy she became a sort of private curse. Frank Lomas was lucky to have been here as long as he had without being called on to declare his partisanship.

'Young man, I need your help.'

There was no star-light of insanity in her eyes as she said those words: no hysteria. She was matter-of-fact, aged but shrewd, in control of herself, husbanding her diminishing strength, but still in command of it.

'Oh, yes?'

She had a reputation for convincing strangers in the opening round.

'Anything that a good neighbour can be called upon to do, ma'am – '

'Yes. You look the kind of man that Margreave can do with.'

'I'm not quite clear, ma'am, what it is you want me to do.'

'I've just told you. You're not going to try to sidle out of it like the rest of them?'

'No, ma'am.'

'There was someone in Badger's again last night.'

As every night for more than half a century, according to her tormented spirit.

'I'll come over some time and look at the place,' he said, incapable of rejecting a pleading woman, even a mad one.

'Now.'

'Not now, ma'am. I have my own work to do.'

She picked up a cobble from the gangue and scratched at a shining facet with her finger-nail.

'It strikes me you are a wasteful young man.'

'All in good time, ma'am. I propose to waste nothing.'

'So when will you come to Badger's? Before tonight?'

'One day soon. Next week, perhaps.'

'That will be too late.'

But he got rid of her: for a while.

And she was not the only one to disappoint him with the sound of her footsteps on the deads. Another time he was lying full length in a confined corner when he heard someone dismount from horse-back and walk towards the mine, unlike Isobel, who did not interrupt him at the face. He wriggled backwards out of his hole and saw that it was Gilbert Slack who was looking at him down the Drift, silhouetted in the daylight of the entrance arch.

'I thought I'd come over and give you a hand, for old time's sake. Got a day off. At least, old Fuller thinks I'm working on the far side of the estate.'

He looked at Lomas's tidy stacks of excavated waste. 'Not much future in building that kind of little wall, is there?'

Then he walked down to the end of the original mine, where the Drift petered out at the end of the founder-miner's hope.

'An extra pair of hands might just do the trick, eh?'

Lomas did not want his assistance, but he was too easy-going and good-natured to say so in that first moment. Slack picked up a shovel and began digging in the gravel at the gallery-end.

'I wasn't going to bother down there,' Lomas said. 'Not until everything else has failed, at any rate. I always reckon the Old Man knew when he was beaten.'

'He couldn't have known more than you and I do,'

Slack said. 'He hadn't got eyes that could see through the stone, had he?'

'I sometimes think he must have had, Gilbert. I'm beginning to think a man needs second sight, to make a living out of a place like this.'

Slack brought out a shovelful of waste and threw it down casually behind him.

'Don't chuck it just anywhere,' Lomas told him. 'Let's keep the place tidy.'

'There's no colonels here, you know, Frank, inspecting your kit lay-out.'

'I don't need any colonel to teach me my job at the rock-face.'

Slack did not answer, but did not alter his way of working, either. Lomas suppressed his anger and crawled back to where he himself had been working. For some minutes he heard the ring of Slack's shovel and the scattering of small stones wherever they happened to fall.

'Don't fret yourself, Frank. If I find what I'm looking for, you can forget about lying on cold stones on your back. I'd not opt for this as full-time work.'

'You'd not opt for full-time work, anyway, would you, Gilbert?'

'That depends on what lies at the end of it.'

Lomas picked up his lamp to inspect a dark line that ran down between the strata. For the thousandth time it was nothing but hard clay, tight-packed under a primeval rock-slide. Gilbert Slack also worked on, a dozen shovelsful, a pause, a curse, then the bite of his blade under the rubble again. Then suddenly he stopped, appeared to be scrabbling in front of himself down amongst the rubbish, flung his shovel angrily up the working and stood astride Lomas's extended legs.

'You bloody rotter! You rotten bloody bastard.'

At first Lomas thought these were the sort of comic tantrums they had sometimes played at in the army, imitating their officers and N.C.Os.

'I don't really think that this is your line of country, Gilbert.'

'Cut out the clever stuff, Lomas. I want to know what's happened to my stuff.'

'What stuff are you talking about?'

'Don't play the bloody innocent, Peg-leg!'

Lomas began to ease himself out of his cranny again and Slack had to step aside for him to manoeuvre. His heavy boot knocked over one of his walls of waste. Slowly and patiently he came out.

'Now – what's all this about?'

'I'll tell you what this is about. That night, in Africa, when I told you there was a fortune waiting in Dead-Nettle –'

'Which I'm beginning to doubt.'

'You? You doubt it? Lomas – when I gave you that piece of information, it was for the sake of whichever of us got here first. On the understanding that it was to be fair shares.'

This, Lomas assured me afterwards, was entirely untrue. No question of sharing had ever been mentioned – or even of any treasure other than crude ore. In any case, Slack had been too drunk, too maudlin, that night in the Transvaal, to remember any of the niceties of their conversation.

'Calm down, Gilbert. I don't know what any of this means.'

'No? You weren't going to dig down there, you said, because that was where the Old Man gave up.'

'I've told you that before.'

'So when *did* you dig down there?'

'Gilbert –'

Slack looked as if he were going to do Lomas violence. But perhaps he remembered that, living or dead, Lomas now held all the court cards, if what he believed about him was true.

'Listen, Lomas. You were discharged before I was. So you got here first. Fair enough. So you did all the hard labour – and why you're still buggering about, pretending to be looking for lead, God above knows. All right: so you want people to think you're on the level, a straightforward lead-getter. Well, you can stand at ease now, Private, sorry, Corporal Lomas, because the betting in Margreave has been that you'd have given up six weeks ago. And all right: you did the bloody work. We'll settle for sixty-forty then. But that's as far as I'll go. Just remember that I did some of the work, too – the real work. And I found myself in the army for my pains – for seven bloody years.'

So that was it. We raked the facts together later: Lomas had not known them. Slack, a reluctant apprentice to the grocery trade – and his father, Tiggy, in a very short while equally reluctant to be his employer: and Gilbert Slack advancing from petty theft to major burglary. We never did work out the full tally. It was too long ago for that, and Slack was obviously not going to tell us. But one particular batch of loot was stashed away in Dead-Nettle. And when Slack was arrested *in flagrante delicto* in some particularly niggardly break-in – he was never a large-scale operator – he came up against one of those judges so unpopular with Her Majesty's military ministers. Gilbert Slack was preserved from a prison sentence on giving his undertaking that he would join the army. It was said in open court that it might make a man of him.

'So where is it, Lomas?'

'I still don't know what you're talking about.'

'Listen, Lomas, let me give you a bit of advice. Don't be in too much of a hurry to try to sell that stuff. Some of it will still be on the lists, even after all this time. Because some of it was bloody good stuff. You want to watch where you try to place it. You'd do better to leave it to the professionals. If *you* get seven years, you'll do them inside. And I do still know a man or two who can help.'

Lomas saw two things clearly. There was something here that he was not going to touch at any price. And Gilbert Slack was about as dangerous a friend as a man could have : Isobel already knew it.

'Somebody must have had your stuff,' he said, 'long before I came on the scene.'

But it angered Slack that Lomas should even try to talk his way out of it.

'Lomas, if you put a foot wrong, I promise I'll see you shopped for it. I'll swear you came with me on the job. You try to pass one item out of that chest, and I'll have every pie-shifter[1] in Derbyshire on watch for you, so help me Christ I will.'

'Come and turn the cottage over,' Lomas said. 'And there's a thousand tons of deads you can shift to one side if you like. Make yourself at home.'

Slack blasphemed. 'So you've had some help to get the stuff off your premises. And you think I don't know who that might be? Well, there's a clear way I can fix you with her for all time. I don't have to tell you what that is. Think it over, Lomas.'

---

[1] Policeman : late nineteenth century underworld slang.

CHAPTER EIGHT

On a third occasion Lomas had to come away from his tunnelling to receive an unexpected caller. This time he was in the middle of a burst of unmusical song when he realised that he was not alone.

> Arse-'ole-diers went to war,
> Arse-'ole-diers won;
> Arse-'ole-diers stuck their bayonets
> Up old Kruger's
> Arse-'ole.

He could not see whether Esmond Fuller thought it shocking or not. He was probably pretending not to have heard, for this morning the landlord looked well kept and respectable, not dressed as he had seen him when he had first called at the Hall, in the floppy comfort of resigned retirement. This was Esmond Fuller business-like and brisk, in tweed hacking jacket and twill riding breeches that were a cut above anything that any other man in Margreave might be wearing. Seeing that he was looking about himself with systematic curiosity, Lomas lit a second lamp and took him on a conducted tour of the little mine, stopping by each of the trial galleries which he had hewn out and since abandoned. He began to explain the strata in somewhat heavy-going detail.

'You can see from this trough-fault that the whole hill-side must have slipped at some time or other. It's in just such a cleft that you might expect to find metal.'

'Only you haven't?'

'No, sir.'

There were in Esmond Fuller's conversation this morning none of the cynical pretences that had charac-terised his talk on the previous occasion. He was not putting on any sort of act this morning, either for Lomas's sake or his own. This was the man who had climbed by his own diligence from nothing to the top of an industrial tree. A courteous man, but one whose soft tongue and courteous manner would not stand in the way of commonsense efficiency. Nor was there anything about him that might let a stranger see how lonely and disillusioning he found the top of the tree to be.

'You've been putting in long hours, Lomas.'

'Yes, sir.'

'It hasn't always been easy for you.' A mere movement of his eyes in the direction of the lame leg.

'No, sir.'

Then a sweeping glance that took in the lines of fastidiously piled debris.

'You work to a system.'

'Yes, sir.'

'So what have you to show for it?'

Lomas was slow to answer. The bottom of his dish was covered now – if he spread out the ore with his fingertips.

'I have some way to go yet, sir.'

'I took the liberty of peeping in at your windows. It looks as if you haven't been idle in the cottage, either.'

Lomas took the hint and let Fuller lead the way out of the mine and across to the building. It belonged, after all, to Fuller; he was entitled to see what had been done with his property. The rent was paid meticulously to the day. No one but Lomas knew what his reserves were. He must have a date in mind beyond which he did not propose to go on labouring here. But even Isobel did not know his mind on this subject.

'You've missed your vocation, Lomas. You ought to be managing a ware-house.'

'I don't want an indoor job, sir.'

'You don't call a hole in the ground indoors, then? But I came to make a suggestion. There are other derelict workings on my estate, dozens of them, in fact. Some of them, to my untutored eye, look a good deal more promising than this one. I'm quite prepared to give you a roving commission. Go prospecting anywhere you like. If you fancy somewhere new to set up shop, by all means take possession. Just let me know what you have in mind, that's all I ask.'

And this was where Lomas showed the fundamental weakness of his temperament. He knew from Slack's revelation that his dreams of Dead-Nettle were founded on nothing. He had come to the point where mere staying-power had become an absurdity. But Lomas still opted to stay.

'Thank you, sir. I'll bear that in mind. I might be glad of it. But I haven't exhausted the possibilities here, and I'm not one for leaving work unfinished. Once I start a job, I like to see it through.'

'As you wish.'

Fuller began to wander round the room, stopped in front of the photographs of Lomas's grand-parental groups. He recognised the ornate gilt frames, and they pulled him up short, but he pointedly said nothing. There was an improbable feminine touch, a posy of dried ever-lasting flowers in a glass vase that Fuller knew he had seen before. There was a pair of brass candle-sticks in the form of cast Grecian figures which had been rescued, it seemed, from a guest bedroom at the Hall.

'I might as well look upstairs while I'm here.'

He helped himself to the creaking rungs of the ladder. Lomas's bed was neatly squared up under a patchwork quilt that had been worked by one of Isobel's great-aunts.

Esmond Fuller rode home in thoughtful mood. That afternoon, for the first time for several weeks, Isobel did not appear at the mine at tea-time. Lomas set a match to his own fire and the potatoes seemed to take an agonisingly long time to come to the boil.

CHAPTER NINE

'What is it that you want from this man?'

And how could she answer that without hurting her father beyond all measure? It would even hurt him to have to acknowledge that there was a gulf between them. They made fun of pretending that there was, and that was their way of escaping from reality. There was a chasm, and it was not of her making or his; she had been determined to find a way of living with it, not to let it part them. She belonged to one world and had to live in another, and the one she belonged to existed nowadays only in the secrecy of her own heart. The situation was bearable only as long as she could dream-live. Had she been a fool to think that they should continue indefinitely like this?

Yet she was determined even now that there was going to be no acrimony between her and her father. He had taken enough knocks.

'What do I want from him? I am not entitled to want anything from him. I don't even know what he wants from himself.'

'You can rule three black lines under that. If he has a mind, he doesn't know it.'

Isobel knew that the danger was that her father might be engendering a totally unjust hatred for Frank Lomas.

She must head him off from that if she possibly could, but her tactics must not be obvious.

'There are plenty of people about,' she said, 'who have no minds. Yet they think they know only too well what is in them.'

'Clever, Isobel – and meaningless. How much longer is he going to go on living on liquidated capital, pursuing an obstinate obsession?'

'I don't know. It's for him to think his own way out of that. It's not for you or me to do his thinking for him. It would be fatal to try to influence him.'

'Yet you do want to influence him?'

'I'd like to help him find himself.'

'Why?'

'Because I think there is something there worth finding. And he needs help of a special kind.'

'Which you think that you can give him?'

'I shall go on trying.'

'Just to amuse yourself?'

'You know me better than that, Father.'

'What, then?'

'I don't know.'

Not by anyone's standards a satisfactory exchange. But her father had managed to keep his temper. He had shown that he still respected her. She felt as if they were over the worst of the confrontation already. She hadn't been explicit with him – but had she ever been explicit with herself on the subject of Frank Lomas? Would this discussion force her to make up her own mind?

'You do know that you're putting yourself in a very dangerous position?' he asked her.

'With Frank? Not that kind of danger, Father.'

He looked as if he had regretted bringing up the subject.

'Maybe he's the one who's in danger,' she countered, and immediately wished she hadn't. The truth about this inevitable row was that they were both too civilised to bring up the things that were really uppermost in their minds. Isobel tried to meet one of these half way and found herself committed to what she had most been hoping to avoid.

'I know what you're thinking. I suppose I can't help disappointing you. I know you gave me an expensive education.'

The Convent: they weren't Roman Catholics, but the place had had the best reputation for academic ambition of any in reach. And then she had gone to a so-called finishing school – in Bruges, of all places. Her mother had felt that that was not so far away from home as Switzerland. It had worked, in that she supposed it had *finished* her, though perhaps not precisely according to the intentions of the twin old-maid principals. Isobel and one or two friends had managed to maintain a common front of their own opinions – in private. Had her true world always been a private one?

'And I'm grateful for all that you did for me. But what am I expected to do now? Marry a Duke?'

'Not at all.'

Her independence of outlook had upset both her mother and father. There had been an immaculate young man with a tailor-made career in private banking who had been put so pointedly in her way that her only defence had been to treat him with contempt: quite unjustly. There had been others – idlers, potential martinets, fawners, butterflies, hypocrites and dullards. It ought to have been a relief to both her parents that she had seen through her suitors. But it sometimes seemed as if they were blaming her for the faults that she found in the men.

79

'I only want you to be happy,' her father said.

A cliché: but he meant it although, paradoxically, he could not possibly know what happiness meant for her. The psychologists were beginning to say that it was the unconscious role of a father to teach a daughter how to love. And then not to let her love? To nourish a passion, and then to forbid it?

'You want to marry this man, Isobel?'

'I've never given such a thing a thought.'

That was a lie, and he went on as if she had said the opposite. 'You mustn't make the mistake of thinking you can change him.'

'I wouldn't want to change him. That would be neither logical nor fair.'

'Nor possible. I've known too many women – and men – who tried to turn their partners into something they couldn't be.'

'I'm not one of those, I hope.'

He remained silent for seconds, taking care not to reject her answers out of hand.

'He doesn't belong to your world,' he said at last.

'What is my world?'

'He isn't an educated man.'

Are you? she wanted to ask. *Was Mother?* Instead, she stayed within bounds.

'What does education mean? Book-learning? Reading fashionable novels? The Grand Tour? He is a considerate, intelligent man.'

'You know nothing of him, really.'

Silence again, both of them thinking. This time Isobel broke in.

'Look, Father, don't let's exaggerate this thing. You must give me credit for at least average prudence. I don't know my own mind, I'll admit. You can't make it up for me, and it would be wrong of you to try. I want to be happy with someone the way you and Mother were happy.'

Dangerous territory. An unfair advantage? If it was social standing that was stinging him, then had he forgotten that both he and her mother had come from working-class terraces?

'I hope, Father, that you're too much of a realist ever to try to stake out a pattern for me. Even if you did, I'm sure you'd be too wise to weep tears if I turned out to be the wrong shape.'

High-minded talk. The only plan that he had for her at the moment was to keep her here as a companion for himself, and that was something to which she had resigned herself. She did not question where her duty lay. It even assured her some measure of freedom. In a great many ways a career could be a bore. She was not entirely an unwilling prisoner at Margreave; but he must not think that he could shackle her spirit too. There was no need for duty to become unpleasant. There might be such a thing as getting the best out of two worlds: the alternative was to get nothing out of either.

'I trust you,' he said. 'I even hate using the word, if it means for a moment that I might not. But I don't want to see you making mistakes that I can help you to avoid. Could I make one or two little points, Isobel? I would hardly call them stipulations. That isn't our way of life. But firstly, you must not take it amiss if I quietly make a few enquiries of my own.'

'If by that you mean pouring strong liquor into Gilbert Slack, I reserve the right to ignore your findings.'

The nearest she ever came to nagging him was over his readiness to listen to Slack. Slack's reminiscences did not impress her. and he had a nauseating habit of showing his scorn for Frank Lomas at every opportunity.

He knew her own movements pretty well, too, and whenever he met her about the grounds he had a way of looking at her that boasted of his knowledge. Her father, on the other hand, firmly claimed that he knew how to manipulate such men. At bottom Slack was a reasonable workman, and with a little jollying along could be kept at the grind-stone. 'The winter will come and go,' Esmond Fuller had said, 'and when the warm weather promises, Slack will be off again. You'll be surprised how much of the work has been done.'

'I certainly do not mean Slack,' he said now. 'There are more reliable sources of information.'

'I'm glad you think so. Slack's friend Harry, for example?'

'Now you are merely being ridiculous. You must leave this to me. I shall be writing one or two confidential letters. You cannot possibly hold that against me. That's point number one. Point number two – '

Her mind jumped away for a moment. At this very time, Frank would be coming out of the mine, finding his cottage cold and comfortless. It was one of those sunless winter twilights and the sky through the window had turned already from dark blue to empty blackness. She could hardly rush out to Dead-Nettle now.

'Point number two: there are certain appurtenances in this house for which I do, it may surprise you to know, cherish a sentimental affection. My pipe-rack, for example. Those two little candle-sticks in Irish bog-oak. And a few other things that perhaps I need hardly enumerate. I don't want to have to move over to Dead-Nettle Drift to enjoy my own possessions.'

Heavily comic, even as to a word like *enumerate*. There was no bitterness in this. It cast his approval on what had already gone over to the mine. She smiled faintly.

'I promise you I'll leave you your bed and bedding,' she said. 'And the things you stand up in.'

'Point number three –'

'Good heavens! Another?'

But this time he wasn't trying to be funny.

'I do think you might find it in your heart to stay home and take tea with me now and then. Shall we say, once a week?'

'Done, Father!'

There were even the beginnings of a nip of guilt here.

'But not on the same day each week, if you don't mind,' she said. 'I hate regular patterns. They make life seem shorter.'

Frank Lomas would soon learn to hate the days when she did not come. And she would school herself sternly. There would be no balsam for either her own impatience or Frank's. On the days when she stayed home to take muffins and toasted tea-cakes with her father, there would be no slipping away to Dead-Nettle at unwonted hours.

'Regularity is a great comfort to some of us,' her father said.

'But you were never one for taking easy ways out were you? Haven't you always refused to sleep on feathers? Don't tell me you've settled for the sybaritic life at last?'

This was more like their normal relationship.

'Not yet,' he said, 'but there might come a time.'

Two or three weeks later, in mid-December, the postman had forecast snow and there were great yellow banks of it building up in the sky over Ranters' Hill. Esmond Fuller went out of his way to be in evidence as she was about to leave the house that afternoon, to warn her that if a blizzard did start, she might find herself weather-bound.

'Now don't try to be selfish, Father. You had your tea-party yesterday.'

'To have one two days running would fill my cup to the brim.'

'And you'd be sure to spill some.'

'Don't say you weren't warned. Once drifting starts in these hills, we can be cut off for days.'

The first flakes began to fall before she reached the mine. Her horse's mane was caked with white crystals as she reined in beside the cottage.

Esmond Fuller had had a premonition that she would not return to the Hall that night. But foreknowledge was no consolation; it did not help him to fall asleep.

CHAPTER TEN

When Esmond Fuller announced that he proposed to make 1904 a Dickensian Christmas, Isobel was mildly delighted that he should be thinking genial thoughts for a change. But when she heard his guest-list, she was filled with the direst foreboding : Frank Lomas, Gilbert Slack, the impervious Harry Burgess and herself : no one from the Margreave world, and no one from their half forgotten blood circle. But there was nothing that she could do about it except to wait in suspense. He had already told them that they were invited, and no force could have persuaded him to give back-word.

When she saw the scale on which he pictured the entertainment, she wondered if advancing age was beginning to unbalance him. He had sent out orders that had enhanced his reputation with local tradesmen and written for hampers from a fashionable mail-order firm : goose and plum pudding, quails and foie gras, ham, tongue and chicken in aspic, petit fours and Mazarines, an instruction down to his own kitchen for a gross of mince-pies. And for strong drink he had laid in port and Madeira, eau de vie, an octavo cask of Vino de Pasto, Chambertin, Musigny, Meursault – and a hogshead of Christmas ale, as if that were for the mere assuaging of casual thirst between courses.

'Father, are you proposing that this party should last a fortnight? You've enough fire-water there to put a regiment to sleep.'

It was the word regiment that was the source of magic for him. Esmond Fuller, the industrialist with a steel spring instead of a heart, was undefended prey when the talk was of Empire and far-flung lines. He had made almost a hobby of Queen Victoria's wars, was as familiar with exotic and desperate corners of the world as if he still had their powder-smoke in his nostrils himself. He used to maintain from his arm-chair that the prosperity of Manchester and the furnaces of the Midlands rested squarely on the men who faced the assegai or groaned with thirst as the life-blood drained from them. Yet he had first-hand knowledge of very few soldiers: which helped him to forgive vagabond opportunists like Gilbert Slack and cloth-headed idlers like Harry, before he had even started to explore them. 'Think what we owe them,' he said, till his words sickened Isobel by their very predictability.

Slack and Harry had spent the second half of Christmas morning in the *Adventurers'* – not drinking heavily by the standards adopted for the day, but returning fairly excitable and red-faced from the brisk air and the festive company. Frank Lomas had already walked over from the mine in a dark suit that was almost pathetic for its self-conscious and humdrum decency, and was facing his host in front of a massive log fire. Isobel, with not very demanding responsibilities for distant over-sight of the kitchen, was sitting with them, sipping from a thimble-glass of sugared water.

It seemed at first as if the men were going to behave themselves. Gilbert Slack, as far as he understood the concept, had evidently decided to be polite. Harry was saying no more than usual, though he had the irritating habit of wriggling his neck in his collar every few minutes or so, which drew attention to his unease in drawing-room garb. Her worst fear for Frank had been that the dominant presence of Slack would subdue him into a bumpkin-like awkwardness. But he seemed to be getting on famously with her father. They were chatting fluently about the fauna of the Veldt.

There had been some change in Gilbert Slack's attitude to her. Her visits to Frank Lomas were no sort of secret and she had not attempted to conceal from anyone that she had spent the night of the blizzard at his cottage. Nor had she shown any embarrassment because everyone knew about it. Her strength on this issue – and I think it cost her a good deal more in nervous energy than most people guessed – was that her father never even began to question her about the occasion. And as far as Gilbert Slack was concerned, it cut from under his feet all possibilities of blackmail. He could no longer be a threat to her, because she was hiding nothing. But she continued to find him offensive. He looked at her always as if he knew, like some old friend, exactly what was going on between her and Frank; as if this was something in which he actually shared her pleasure – and as if he felt sure that he had only to wait his own turn.

They drank Christmas ale, thick, fruity and sweet, on top of whatever else they had imbibed, and sat down at table at about three o'clock in the afternoon, still in an atmosphere of exaggerated respect for each other, though noisier now than any of them realised, including her father. There was a flush over his cheek-bones that she had never seen there before, and he plied the men with mountains of food as if he were experimenting for some purpose of his own to see how much he could press into them.

And at the same time, he was pushing them into military reminiscences.

'I suppose your officers did their best at Christmas time, wherever you happened to be, to introduce something of the festive spirit?'

'*Officers!*'

Esmond Fuller was tolerant about their contempt for their leaders; he did not, clearly, believe it to be justified, but he treated it nevertheless as something that he expected and that amused him. Gilbert Slack, as far as a full mouth and the tricky enunciation of the words permitted, tried to be explicit – and portentous.

'No, actually, sir, our officers: well, Major Aspinell we'd have followed anywhere, and did. But for the most part they were just a social club, a race apart, you might say. They knew very little of what was going on in the ranks, and wouldn't have been able to do anything about it if they did. It was the N.C.O.s who held the army together.'

Fuller turned towards Lomas.

'And you were an N.C.O.'

'Aye – the *janker-wallah* corporal.'

This was from Harry, fully drunk now, emboldened and foolish. His tactlessness earned him a perceptible nudge from Slack; but too late. He had aroused Fuller's interest.

'What does that mean, *janker-wallah* corporal? I

thought that *jankers* was a term taken over from the Indian Army, and that it meant men under punishment. Am I to understand that Frank was in charge of disciplining defaulters?'

'Yes, that's it,' Slack began, still eager, from some strategy of his own, to see the peace kept. But Lomas stepped in with his own blundering sense of honesty.

'What they are trying to tell you is that I was given my stripes by accident.'

He proceeded to tell a story which had the others in fits of laughter, though he did not smile himself.

It had happened just after Colenso, one of the first major defeats of the campaign, and one that shattered the confidence of that segment of British society that understood it. The battalion was in disarray, still collecting its stragglers, its uniforms torn and caked with mud, the soles half torn off its boots, its rations late and decimated, water in short supply.

Lomas, as was by no means infrequent in his service, was at that time a convicted defaulter for some minor misdemeanour. He had had a penchant for unwitting disciplinary offences since his earliest recruit days, was prone to be caught red-handed in every 'crime' he committed, and was the natural scapegoat for two thirds of the sergeants and corporals in his company. As a man under punishment he came regularly into the particular province of the Provost-Sergeant, a past master in the art of the intolerable. The Provost-Sergeant had brought with him all the way from their barracks at home an old bucket and a length of iron chain which were kept rusting in water in the day-time, to be brought up to a high polish in their off-duty hours by the men confined to barracks. In action, the most obnoxious of fatigues were always reserved for these miscreants. And one of the Provost-Sergeant's most

88

subtle tortures was to have his *janker-wallahs* parade before him every half-hour, on each occasion with some laborious variant of uniform or equipment. A full, finnicky lay-out of every item in a man's kit, five minutes before Lights Out, was one of his favourites.

Lomas suffered it all with what must have amounted to a bovine resignation. He knew what it was to have a period of *jankers* prolonged for slothful compliance. The Provost-Sergeant, catching sight of him in the chaotic *laager* after Colenso, had suddenly ordered him to appear before him in a quarter of an hour in full ceremonials.

Then on the scene came General Sir Redvers Henry Buller, a veteran of the Chinese War of 1860, a V.C. against the Zulus – the man who, some have said, originally and personally invented spit and polish. The state of the battalion disgusted him : a dirty soldier was a potential coward. Bayonets were not made to be camouflaged in ambush : they were meant to flash in the sun. And in the middle of his searing reprimand of Lomas's commanding officer, he spotted Lomas, standing at attention beside the improvised guard-compound, in his red tunic, with ball-buttons of apparently pure gold, a knife-edge crease actually sewn into his blue patrol trousers, his number one boots brought up to a mirror-like shine by the extraction of all grease from the leather with the handle of a hot spoon.

'Now, there's something like a soldier.'

And he ordered Lomas to be made a Queen's Corporal on the spot, a substantive rank *honoris causa* from which nothing less than a court martial could demote him.

'But sir, this man is a defaulter.'

'What does that matter ? A man isn't a soldier until he has shown that he can take field punishment.'

So Lomas became a further embarrassment to his

commanders in the most unexpected way. What was to be done with him now? Harry had the answer. Although he was still not drunk enough to say the words aloud in front of Isobel, he mouthed them silently for the sake of Frank and Gilbert.

'*Shit-wallah.*'

They had made Lomas Sanitary Corporal. He had been put in charge of the small band of camp-scavengers, latrine diggers and night-soil disposers.

'They say an army marches on its stomach,' Gilbert Slack began to say.

'You mean that Frank was a cook?'

'Not exactly. In the same line of business, you might say, only further down the line.'

'I don't understand.'

Isobel did. She had already coaxed this part of Frank's story out of him in her own way.

'I think we've heard enough of this,' she said.

'As a matter of fact,' her father intervened, 'by a coincidence I have just been having a correspondence with Frank's former commanding officer over quite a different matter – and what he has to say about his qualities as a soldier are so glowing that it might be an embarrassment for him to hear them in company. And you, sir – '

He addressed himself in a not unkindly manner to Slack, but with a firmness that even in his state of inebriation, Slack could not miss.

'You, sir, should be the last man to poke fun at a comrade-in-arms. It is acknowledged in despatches that he saved your life.'

'That's true, sir,' Slack conceded. 'And for that reason – '

For that reason, driven into shrill, hysterical high spirits by the secondary shock, the delayed reactions of terror and relief, Slack had promised Lomas treasures untold if ever he could make his way back to Dead-Nettle Drift. In the long hours of that dark night, cut off from their main body, waiting for the dawn before they could know whether there was any salvation for them, he had talked wildly and with maudlin sentiment about Margreave and the wealth to be wrested from its hills.

'You've been a miner, Frank. Those buggers up there have all given up trying. You could make the fortune of a life-time in three years, if you were prepared to stick it out. And it wouldn't be like those old coal-pits of yours. Not in any way.'

Lomas had fastened on to it like a vision.

'And he had to kill a woman to do it,' Harry said, belatedly, the topic almost already talked out. The drink seemed to be fuddling Harry into a new kind of pride, a pride in being the bringer of scandalous news.

'Remember the look on her face, Frank?'

'What does it matter whether it was a man or a woman?' Slack said. 'When she's got the butt of a Mauser to her shoulder, there are some things you don't worry over-much about.'

'You mean she was a partisan?' Fuller asked, disconcerted at an unromantic aspect of heroism.

'I think we've all had enough of this story,' Isobel announced. 'When you take things out of their context, you do justice to no one. I'm quite sure – '

But she did not in fact know what she was quite sure about. She stole a look at Frank, the fringe of familiar beard, the huge honest face, the clear suggestible eyes. Was it true that he had killed a woman? In cold blood? It was plain, as Slack said, that war was war, and if someone was pointing a gun at you – or your friend –

then chivalry obviously went low on your list. Even if the friend was Gilbert Slack.

All the same, if you had killed a fellow creature, were you ever the same?

'And there's another thing we ought to ask Frank – '

Harry again. The sooner he drank himself insensible –

'We ought to ask Frank – '

Gilbert Slack and Esmond Fuller leaned forward simultaneously across the table to silence him – but it was the older man, suddenly, unexpectedly authoritative, yet without a spoken word, who did the trick. Harry seemed to slump in his place.

And Frank Lomas suddenly felt sobered and cold. Could this imply that Isobel's father knew? Or had this just been some shaft of his managerial intuition? Had his commanding officer seen no need for personal discretion in his letter to Fuller? Or had Gilbert Slack, who could not sit on blackmail evidence for ever, already opened his weak and evil mouth?

Frank tried to persuade himself that if the old man already knew, then he would not be sitting here as a guest at his table. Then Isobel got up and quite unnecessarily went down to visit the kitchen. The cook and her assistants were now sipping Marsala and eating mincepies. Isobel stayed and gossiped with them. When she returned to the dining-room, the men were all laughing together, raucous, undisciplined, no differences now. They did not seem aware that she had come back into the room, so she side-stepped out again, went up to her bedroom and began writing 'thank you' letters for presents from relatives who seemed now to belong to a detached existence.

An hour and a half later, coming down to offer – she did not know whether there was any sense in it – to make a pot of tea, she found them all asleep: her father slumped sideways at the head of the table still, Harry with the side of his face in a plate of congealed goose-fat, Lomas and Slack in the two fireside chairs.

I think that Frank might have found it difficult to repair himself in her esteem, had not her father remained equally incapable for the remainder of the day. As it was, she largely blamed the old man for the whole range of stupid events. But she spared him direct rebuke. It would have been superfluous. On Boxing Day he was a contrite and seedy man. Slack and Harry kept wisely out of sight. She did not go over to Dead-Nettle. But the day after, she went there again – and Christmas was not mentioned.

There is much that remains unclear about the three months that followed. There were things that a man and a woman could not be expected to speak of – and could perhaps not be relied upon if they did.

The cottage at Dead-Nettle was far from its apogee of neatness and care when I came to see it, and it certainly did not strike me at first as an ideal love-nest. But, after all, it is not rush-matting and great-auntly bed-spreads that make the nest. There was much snow that winter, and it did not always play into the couple's hands, as on the night of that first blizzard. Sometimes they were frustrated: Isobel was incarcerated in the Hall. Once this lasted a fortnight, and at the first signs of thaw – she was so inexperienced in the vagaries of Low Peak weather that she did not know that going conditions could be even more treacherous in melting snow than over frozen drifts – she rode out to Dead-Nettle with no effort to dissimulate her sense of urgency.

At some point during those weeks, Lomas made his rational decision to give up his battle against the rock. I do not know whether this was gradual or finally sudden. I do not think that Isobel encouraged him; but nor did she allow him to have second thoughts. Untypically, I do not think he had any idea what he would do next; for the moment, I do not think he cared. I do not believe that either of them cared. He was not without some choice – and spring, when it came, would be the time for choosing. They reclined into a haven of timelessness and did not let other things matter.

Then spring began to advertise itself as a reality. Coltsfoot flowered and went to seed amongst the gangue, celandines in the moister earth of the bank of a rill. One afternoon in March when Isobel came to the mine, she found the place deserted and the padlock on the cottage door hanging like a leaden seal that seemed to be ordering her away. There was no sign anywhere of Frank. He had left no kind of message. The nearest neighbour was old Florence Belfield, and she was unlikely to know anything.

It was on the evening of that day that Lomas, uncaring for traffic, walked down the middle of a Derby street, advancing to meet the woman in crushed strawberry and green whose aspect seemed, according to bystanders, to bring him surprisingly little joy. A man and two women held fast to the shadows in which they had been waiting to ambush her.

Three days later I was sent to Margreave in my official capacity.

CHAPTER ELEVEN

We had no grave difficulty in reconstructing Frank Lomas's evening in Derby. A little conventional ground-work and we were in a position to be specific. At 8.01 p.m. on Thursday, 24 March 1905, he arrived by a slow passenger train from Wirksworth, three minutes behind tabled time. He had been one of the last out of the carriage and had clumped along the platform like a man uncertain of his surroundings, having to look for the Way Out sign and appearing to have forgotten that he would be asked at the barrier for his ticket, which he then had some difficulty in finding, though it was in the obvious place in his waistcoat pocket. From the Entrance Hall he had stood looking for some moments of indecision, as if the size and shapelessness of the town not merely confused, but actually offended him. Our informant on this nicety was the cabby whom he turned back to ask for direction to St Mary's Gate, and to whom he showed a slip of paper with the address of Hetty Wilson's lodging written on it. It was now 8.10 precisely: the cabby looked at the clock, because he was to pick up a fare on the 8.09 from Burton-on-Trent. Lomas obviously did not loiter on his way across the town. We know that P.C. Kewley had met his Sergeant in Irongate at 8.37, as recorded in both their note-books, and it was at 8.44 exactly, according to the constable, that he had moved across to part the crowd round a dying horse in Edward Street. So it must have been between 8.39 and 8.41 that Lomas met Hetty Wilson in the middle of the road, close under the eyes, though unaware of them, of Tilly Sutcliffe, Martha Lang and Duncan Mottershead.

We were proud of our precision, and it did our machine good to be put through its motions; but it was all relatively uninformative. If only someone could have told us a single phrase that passed between the pair of them. The ticket inspector who reported Lomas's exit from the platform described him as a man with something on his mind. The cabby said that he had seemed shy of asking his way, as if the address on the piece of paper were something to be ashamed of. Tilly Sutcliffe, when I pressed her over a second port and lemon, came out with the information that Hetty Wilson had seemed overjoyed to see him, but that he had simply stood looking at her as a drawing-room cat might curl his lip away from a dish of stale food. The cabby, whose gentleman from Burton-on-Trent had not appeared, and who was now waiting on the off-chance of custom from the Manchester express, saw them arrive back at the station a little after nine o'clock. Lomas was carrying the woman's Gladstone bag, but they were walking with a gap of a foot or so between them: a striking couple, she in her musical comedy crushed strawberry, he self-consciously dark and sober, his four-soled boot stumping heavily in the comparatively deserted Waiting Hall.

But weren't they talking at all? Wasn't there a soul amongst those who had seen them who had heard them exchange a word?

They had over half an hour to wait for the next train to Wirksworth. Lomas bought the woman a cup of tea and an iced currant bun. He took nothing himself. The attendant at the refreshment counter did not hear anything that either of them said. They seemed close, in that they appeared to want to keep themselves apart from other travellers, yet distant in that when she made a move to take his arm, he gave the impression of want-

ing to thrust her aside. *Demure, brazen, pretty, delicate,*
coarse, coquettish, shy : these were all adjectives that
appeared in our notes of people's impressions. And
Lomas's mood was severally described as *moody, digni-*
fied, surly, anxious, aloof, pre-occupied, proud and
distraught. Once murder was out, observers took their
particular sides, and saw what they wanted to see.

They shared a compartment on the train as far as
Duffield, had only each other for company thereafter.
At Wirksworth he had waiting for them the same hired
cart which he had borrowed to bring his load of furniture to Dead-Nettle. It was open to the elements and bore
no trace of upholstery. The charred wicks of its lamps
did no more than cast flickering pools of light on the
undulating verges. I asked the late-night porter who had
locked up the station after them whether the woman
had appeared in any way to protest at the crudeness
of their transport. He said that she had taken half a
step backwards in shock and dismay, but that Lomas
had appeared not to notice the gesture. He swung her
bag on to the boards and left her to clamber up as best
she could over the shafts. When, however, she let out
a little whimper to tell him that she was in extreme
difficulty, with her heel caught up in her skirts behind
her, he did move to help her with one hand under her
elbow. He lifted her up to the front of the cart – there
was no seat – and there, it seemed, she was going to be
likely to have to remain, unless another moment of
passing chivalry eventually moved him to help her down
again. He mounted beside her, signalled to her that she
would have to move her body sideways to make room
for his outstretched leg, twitched the reins and sent them
cantering out of such nocturnal light as remained in
the town.

Margreave did not fall over itself to bear witness

to their arrival. It must have been well after eleven by the time they were on the final road to Dead-Nettle. I did not doubt that more than one pair of eyes was drawn to the edge of the bedroom curtains by the sound of wheels and hooves at that hour. But no one came forward to talk about it.

There was one event, however, that came to light as if by community accord. Dead-Nettle was a long way from other habitations, yet Margreave, to its last soul, was aware that the iron-rimmed wheels had crunched through the cat dirt outside the Drift, that Lomas had unlocked the door of his cottage for the woman, lit the lamp for her inside, then come out alone to un-harness and stable the cob. After a short while he had gone indoors again, and for a long while the pale light behind the living-room curtains which Isobel Fuller had hung was visible across the slag. Lomas possessed only one lamp, and he must have picked it up to show the woman up the ladder. It was the bedroom window that now showed across the deads.

Silence then, emphasised by the normal rustles of the night, whilst the watcher who brought this piece of news back to the village waited for the extinction of the light and whatever thoughts that moment might inspire in him.

But the light remained behind the bedroom window for a long time – a long time, that is, in view of the fact that lamp-oil was expensive and Lomas was known to be a thrifty man. Then suddenly the night was pierced by a long series of screams from that upper room – the shrieking of a terrified and hysterical woman, cutting like a broken-edged knife across the empty shadows of Whim Hill.

I am in considerable doubt as to whether even such noise as this was declared to be could possibly have penetrated to many who claimed to have heard it. Yet all Margreave seemed to be able to give a personal account of it. It was not an individual report, it was a community rumour, established as a legend by half way through the next morning.

During the course of my investigations, I came across only one description that had the freshness of conviction behind it – and that from the one witness who had not known who or what it might have been – old Florence Belfield, the miner's widow, who lived in her own nightmare galleries of yesterday's misery, who heard it and thought that someone was being murdered for some ancient treachery of internecine miner's strife. She did not come forward about it immediately. By the time that she did, she had been able to embroider it with at least half a dozen possible explanations, all of them absurd, and some of them in conflict with each other. But somehow I found her account more impressive than the prosaic common story current in the village. Florence Belfield said that they were the cries of a woman who draws a curtain in a closet to find the eyeless sockets of death within inches of her face.

But the next morning, Friday, 25 March, the woman we have hitherto known as Hetty Wilson was not dead. She appeared in the village, admittedly looking round herself with the uncertainty to be expected from a stranger, but without unease, and certainly without the humility which people, in all circumstances, felt that they had the right to expect of her. She behaved as if she knew that she had every right to be there, and to be served by the tradespeople without question or comment; as, by and large, she was, so metallic was her confidence. She bought cottons and a packet of needles at Matty Cooper's little drapery and a single penny stamp from the acidulous Old Fan at the Post Office. Then she went over to Tiggy Slack's grocery and, looking with critical curiosity round the shelves whilst waiting customers were served, eventually ordered sugar, flour, Snowflake biscuits, Carlsbad wafers, French stoneless cherries, jellied meats in glass jars. Whatever of the exotic had penetrated into Margreave, she chose as her own. She asked if her order could be delivered to the mine.

It could not. It was the satisfaction of Tiggy Slack's life to plead that he had not bought his errand-boy a new bicycle to have its frame shaken to pieces riding over scree. Hetty sweetly said that she would arrange for the things to be called for.

'And put them down to the account,' she said.

Frank Lomas did not have a credit account. He paid, a few pence at a time, for everything he bought. But Tiggy Slack did not demur. My private opinion is that it would have delighted his heart to be able to pass around the word that Frank Lomas was a bad debtor. It would have been worth the debt.

'With pleasure, Mrs – ?'

'Mrs Lomas,' she said, evidently surprised that he did not know.

CHAPTER TWELVE

Saturday, 26 March:
A.m.: Hetty Lomas appeared again in the Market Square in Margreave, bought one or two small things at Slack's: half a pound of butter, lambs' tongues in aspic, a packet

of Abernethy biscuits. Her method of shopping was to buy things as they caught her eye, and in small quantities. Evidently she had never kept house according to a plan.

Next she went again to the drapery, bought curtain material: printed art muslin with a cherry-coloured trefoil device. Old Matty Cooper tried to save her pennies by getting her to be precise about lengths, widths and selvedges, but she did not seem to have taken measurements, except with her eyes.

'About half as long again as the brass rule along the counter-top – no, quarter as long.'

But she had certain qualities, a pouting lip and a pleading eye, that affected even as static an observer as old Matty Cooper. He was like a man running races with himself to help her. She smiled, both with evident enjoyment of this for its own sake, and because she saw him for what he was: another man.

'If she *is* his wife – and she's wearing a ring,' he said to his own wife afterwards, 'it's a shame he's brought her up here to live in a hovel like that.'

Outside the shop she caught the eye of Gilbert Slack who, for once without Harry, was examining bib-and-brace overalls on a market stall. An unbiased eavesdropper (and, to be sure, there was one – within days I was talking to that bib-and-brace salesman) might have formed the impression that the pair were strangers to each other. She began to finger through a pile of dungarees, and they carried on a conversation without facing up to each other.

'So you've not brought him round yet?'

'He'll come,' she said. 'But it will be a long business. He's an obstinate swine.'

'But you know your stuff, Hetty. You used to, anyway.'

The bib-and-brace man moved away to a further corner of his stall – but not so far as to risk losing any of this.

'It just happens that the man I am married to is the one who doesn't want it.

'And listen, Gil – you owe me something, after that doss-house in Derby.'

'We had to get him to fetch you, Hetty. There was reason behind that. If you'd arrived out of the blue, he could have turned you away. And there's another thing: coming to fetch you from away – it shows folks he wants you, doesn't it?'

'Wants me!'

'He had to break a meeting with his lady-love to go and meet you.'

'You've told her I'm here?'

'*I* haven't. But she's heard rumours. Fruity ones. I've taken good care of that.'

'And how has she taken it.'

'Mad as a cat.'

'Just let's get this all over. She can have him back, and welcome. If I could only get him off my shadow for an hour. I daren't start looking. I never know when I'm going to hear that foot clumping over the step.'

'I'll see to it for you. Tomorrow night. He always goes in the evening to his Chapel service. You make sure he does. And don't go with him.'

'Ta.'

'The moment he's out of the house, get to work. Look for freshly turned flooring, loose stones in the wall, hollow places behind the chimney breast. I'll guarantee he won't be home before midnight.'

Saturday, 26 March:
P.m.: Lomas had a new interest. For some time now,

facing up to the reality that there was no fortune, not even an existence for him out of the lead, he had thought of developing the sparse but certainly under-used farming potential of his small-holding.

He knew nothing about farming. There was no clear-cut plan in his mind. To fatten a few beef-cattle, perhaps? To build a sty and rear pigs? Whatever he might scratch from the land, it was clear that he must first make good his dilapidated boundaries. The wall at the lower end of his rough pasture was in poor repair. To be out and mending it was a reasonable occupation for a Saturday afternoon in spring.

Besides, he found life in the cottage with that woman unendurably claustrophobic.

The first thing that struck Isobel Fuller as she rode up to the mine was that the curtains that she had made had been taken down. The blank window-panes seemed to be gaping at her across the slag like eyes sightless in death. It was not, of course, that Hetty had worked any miracles with the material she had bought this morning. She had done no more than unwrap it and lay out her needles and thread on the table, ready to start. But it had been an act of compulsion to pull down the old ones as soon as Frank was out of the house.

She opened the door to Isobel and knew at once who she was. Frank had said very little about the woman whose touch was so obvious about his home. And although Hetty could not, from one circumstance or another, be said ever to have known him well, she was adept at reading any man's silences. She could not, by any twisting of psychological subtleties, be said to have been in love with Frank Lomas, either now or at any other time, but she was not prepared to countenance the competition of those curtains. They seemed to stress his contempt for her; for although she did not love him.

and did not want to, she expected him to show some signs of being moved by her. She was galled by that stiff-backed sense of moral duty with which he showed that he was prepared to tolerate her; only because he thought he must. She writhed at the unfeeling courtesy with which he thought himself obliged to treat her. There was a type of man, she knew only too well, who scorned her; but Frank Lomas had no right to consider himself in that class. He had not scorned her once; he had wanted her badly enough to marry her.

The sight of Isobel, framed in the doorway, was like seeing an embodiment of those curtains. Hetty had expected someone who fancied herself a lady; she saw here a woman who possessed all the things that she herself would never have – and not material things, at least, not only material things. It was not merely Isobel's natural poise, nor the fact that she was clearly conscious of it. It was something she seemed to parade.

Isobel saw the material on the table and her own curtains ignominious in a heap on the floor. And there is nothing more remarkable than the manner in which two women of widely differing quality and aspirations can immediately see into the depths of each other's motives and vulnerability. And nothing can be more devastating than a skirmish between them, with all the preliminaries taken for granted. They are like two chess-players who know each other's game so well that they might as well start with an almost empty board.

Isobel Fuller, looking at Hetty Lomas against the background of the home which she herself had done so much to create, almost held her breath. She was determined not to lose her aplomb. For a few seconds, it looked as if Hetty was going to be the one to break down.

'Yes?'

A spate of vulgar abuse was not far beneath the surface.

'I've come for the rent, if you please.'

'Rent? I shall have to ask my husband.'

They stood and looked at each other. Hetty, not having taken the trouble over her face that she had judged worthy of the back-streets of Derby, no longer looked eighteen. Some suggestion of her true history was to be read in pores that had been clogged for most of her adult life. Even the whites of her eyes seemed to Isobel sluggish. She hoped that the last two sleepless nights would not be apparent in her own face.

'There's no need for that. If you'll excuse me a moment –'

Isobel took a step into the room, to such purpose that Hetty, whose first instinct was to defend the hearth with tooth and claw, moved aside to let her in.

Isobel put up her hand to the mantel-shelf and lifted down the rent-book without disturbing the pile of receipts on which it lay.

'May I? I know where he keeps it.'

She reached for the old biscuit-tin in the shape of a lantern with a conical lid, emptied three shillings and four pennies into the palm of her hand and held the sum out for Hetty to see. Then she signed the receipt in the book with a silver propelling pencil from her handbag and held out the page also for examination. Hetty turned her eyes away, as if it were beneath her to show interest in the transaction. She left Isobel to stretch up and put back the rent-book where she had found it, and in doing so, this time she dislodged one of the other papers, which fluttered down to the rug. She picked it up and put it back, making an exaggerated movement with her eyes to make sure she could not be accused of trying to read private business. (She knew the paper well enough. It was one of Frank's sketches of tools for the blacksmith.)

'That's all you'll be wanting, then?'

Like the inhabitants of Derby, Isobel was unable to place Hetty's accent. She classified it merely as *common*.

'That's all I am wanting. You would not challenge my right to collect my father's rent.'

'You come for it every week at this time?'

Isobel felt an insane desire to laugh. She had been coming more or less every day, and usually had to be reminded to take the rent when it was due.

'We can no doubt think of some other arrangement, if you prefer.'

Hetty shrugged her shoulder. To show that she did not care, that was the nearest to an insult that she could offer. Isobel stood for a moment, waiting to see whether anything else needed to be said. But Hetty's eyes shifted back to the work waiting for her on the table. Isobel turned and walked away from the cottage. She did not close the door behind her, and Hetty made no move towards it. It seemed unfamiliarly hard going, walking across the slag towards her horse. After she had ridden some fifty yards from the mine, she heard the door closed, roughly and rudely. She did not look back over her shoulder.

She was usually able to come and go from the Hall without bothering her father with her movements. Today, however, it was her luck that he should come out of his room as her foot was on the stairs. She turned to speak to him, and he was shocked by the weariness in her. She opened her bag and gave him the three shillings and four-pence.

'I'm sorry, lass. There's nowt else I can say.'

When he was deeply moved, he had a habit of lapsing

into the speech of his indigenous Lancashire. It did at least appear to simplify issues. Today she felt that it was the one thing calculated to break her heart.

CHAPTER THIRTEEN

Sunday, 27 March:
Evening: As usual, Lomas went to Chapel. As usual he took his seat in a side-pew at the back, amongst men whom by now he knew well by sight, but with whom he had not struck up a deeper acquaintance.

> *One more day of reaping o'er,*
> *One more sheaf to crown our store,*
> *One sweet hour to bathe the soul,*
> *Here in the streams of joy that roll.*

Unusually, his abrasive tenor did not dominate the singing tonight. As a matter of form he had his hymn-book open, but not at the right place. Once, he sat down before the beginning of the last verse, so little was he aware of what was going on. And there was something in the sermon – on the text *Can a man take fire in his bosom and his clothes not be burned?* – that either offended or emotionally upset him, for he stood up in the middle of it and clumsily eased his way past the knees in the pew, out into the grey and deserted street : half an hour at least before he might have been expected to have appeared there. Perhaps that was why Gilbert Slack did not, as he had promised Hetty, meet him at the chapel door to take him off somewhere until well after midnight. Or perhaps Gilbert Slack had thought better of the rendezvous, and felt that two pairs of hands might make lighter work in the miner's cottage? That was one of the things we were left to find out.

And Gilbert Slack was not the only one who claimed to have intended to meet Lomas after the service. That was the reason given by Isobel Fuller, when we called on her to account for why she was wandering disconsolate about the hills, at an advanced hour of the night. Knowing Frank's habits, she said, she had proposed to confront him at that quiet hour. She was going to compel him to explain himself and his appalling treatment of her. Yet she did not want to blame him entirely until she had heard all that lay at the back of it. She knew Lomas well, his strengths and his weaknesses. She knew there were moral dilemmas before which he might become immobilised; though she might see her way through the same problem in a second. Why had he never told her of this marriage? If it was a marriage? She knew; she did not know. She wanted to know; she did not want to know. She never wanted to see him again; she had to see him again. Isobel Fuller, when first we tried to talk to her, was no paragon of clarity. She was being so cruelly pulled in opposite directions that something must surely give under the strain – if it had not already done so.

But she was a brave woman – or at least she wanted to persuade herself that she was. At bottom she was a reasonable one. I did not yet know her well enough to know where the truth lay, but I determined at the outset not to close my mind to the possibility that she was telling the truth on one issue: that she had indeed meant to give Lomas this one chance to explain himself.

It was in character that she should sink her pride to do what seemed just.

But when Lomas did not come out of Chapel with the rest, she was assailed by one principal thought: that the hold of this woman was so strong over him that for her he would even forsake his religious observances – which she respected, though they meant nothing to her personally. It was a deep-dyed mood that prevailed in her. She saw only blackness, and went off into the dark countryside, so she told us, to try to think things out, to refashion her view of the future.

She did not tell us then, in that opening interview, that she was pregnant. That only came to light later. And I am inclined to believe that Lomas did not know it until I told him myself. So perhaps that was what she really wanted to tell him as they walked together that night out of the quiet Sunday village.

But Frank Lomas, too, went off in a fugue into the hills. *The hills*, as he told us, *whence cometh my help*. He was still in a state of repetitive and confused religious fervour when first we talked to him.

Little help did actually come to him in his wanderings over damp fields and through dark woods, but out of those hills came yet another unexpected visitor to the *Adventurers' Arms*. The usual knot of men were sitting in their usual seats, talking their usual talk and lapsing into their usual silences when a commotion at the door let in the wild and hag-like figure of Florence Belfield. Not one of them had ever seen her in the inn before, in fact they had long since given up thinking of her as capable of intelligible communication. But tonight she was so genuinely and frighteningly upset that some-one eventually put a glass of brandy into her fingers, fortified by which she succeeded at last in telling some sort of story.

At first it seemed like one of her usual tales. She still believed that she was running her late husband's mine, and that most of the derelict galleries around her were being worked by gangs hostile to her. Tonight there had been a fight on the forefield – the actual working face of her mine – a foray such as had happened more than once in her youth. She believed that her holding was being attacked by the new man at Dead-Nettle. Some of the regulars were beginning to laugh, but the mention of Dead-Nettle brought some attention. Over to Dead-Nettle she had plodded, her mid-century mourning skirts sweeping the slag, and she had found Dead-Nettle ablaze with light, the windows uncurtained, the door staring open, a woman screaming. Then the screaming had stopped, horses' hooves had ridden off. Florence Belfield was barely articulate when she tried to explain what she had found there. But she opened a fold in her skirts and showed the *Adventurers'* inhabitants blood; not a smear, not a spattering, but a soaked patch that still clung stickily. Ghosts there may be in Florence Belfield's life; but ghosts do not bleed.

'We'd better get over there.'

That was how the men from the pub came upon the body of Hetty Lomas, a sight appalling to see. It looked at first as if she had been trying to prise stones out of the inside wall and had started a minor avalanche that had crushed in her skull. Broken stone lay everywhere; blood and brains were soaked into the limestone dust like purple gruel. Then someone saw one of Frank Lomas's custom-built iron wedges, and it looked as if that, too, had been buried deep in her cranium.

So the men from the *Adventurers'* undertook their own tour of the hills, and brought in severally, for custody by their constable, the various people they found who claimed to be seeking inspiration from benighted nature. There were Gilbert Slack and his friend Harry Burgess, who said that they had their master's authority to take rabbits by night; though it was not rabbit's blood, judged by quantity alone, that made caked patches on Slack's trousers. They found Isobel Fuller, looking outwards from the wall coping of a spinney, the light of incipient madness in her eyes. And they found Frank Lomas, with blood on his boots, muttering that the Lord above was mightier than the noise of many waters.

The next morning I came into the story in my own right.

CHAPTER FOURTEEN

For custody by their constable –

There was pathetically little that P.C. Newton could have done single-handed. He was a country version of P.C. Kewley at Derby – about the same age, too, though he looked older. And slower moving; he was deliberate, but inexorable; a man who did not often emerge from the hills. He had found that in his experience tomorrow always did come – and that there had been time to do then, with calm judgement, some of the things that he might have botched yesterday.

Custody? He could not arrest them all, and he had no reliable holding charge, even against the one whom he must obviously regard as culprit. Surveillance was beyond his resources: but it was not beyond the resources of the unpredictable men of Margreave. If any single one of the suspects – Frank Lomas, Gilbert Slack,

Florence Belfield or Isobel Fuller – had clearly been guilty, then that mob might well have shown an ugly disposition. But there was safety in uncertainty, for once. Constable Newton acted as catalyst while vigilante guards for the night were mounted over the various homes.

Newton had also this in common with Kewley, that he had hoarded over the years suspicions on which it would have been premature, tactless or primitively unjust to have acted. In the heart of that night after the killing of Hetty Lomas, he made painstaking, eloquent notes – primarily memoranda for his own guidance, to try to get some order into the things that he knew I would be asking.

My first job was to try to get some order, too – into the filth and detritus in the cottage at Dead-Nettle, to have the corpse taken away and arrangements made for the surgeons to report on it. Lomas had been shut up for the night in the frightful, stinking hovel, guarded by sentries inside and out, shouldering farm-yard tools and ancient sporting musketry. I dismissed them and brought Lomas out into the morning sunshine on his waste-tip. He was dazed and unwashed. He hardly seemed to grasp who I was. And his mind was still running through his store of half digested texts.

'*He that is surety for a stranger shall surely smart for it.*'

'Yes,' I said.

We sat on the wreckage of the mine's old crushing wheel. I sent other people away.

'Cause and effect, Mr – ?'

'Brunt. Inspector in the detective department of the county constabulary.'

'Cause and effect, Mr Brunt. *For I am a stranger with thee, and a sojourner as all my fathers were.*'

I let him drivel on for a few minutes – at the same time casting my eye over P.C. Newton's notes.

LOMAS, Frank: Formerly coal-miner and discharged wounded soldier; came to Margreave last September with obsession to work old lead-mine. Former acquaintance of G. SLACK, who seems to have exerted an unusually strong influence on him throughout his adult life.

SLACK, Gilbert: Involved in robberies about this district in his youth. Accepted army service as alternative to term of imprisonment. Other burglaries of which he was suspected included Moorbridge Hall, Stores at Youlgreave and offices at Hurdlow Quarries. Commonly believed to have hidden the proceeds of some of his felonies locally. Possibility that Dead-Nettle Drift was one of his caches.

Question: Did Lomas come upon his wife rifling a hoard in the cottage while she thought him at Chapel?

Question: What connection between Lomas's wife and his and Slack's common past?

Suggestion: Slack's constant companion, Harry Burgess, is unintelligent and has been known to be indiscreet. More likely than Slack to be careless under questioning.

FULLER, Miss Isobel: Daughter of manor. Settled in Margreave with her father less than two years ago. Appears to have become infatuated with Lomas. Compromising overnight stay at mine-cottage; justified by weather conditions, but free and unconventional relations seem since to have become a habit.

'*O spare me a little that I may recover my strength,*' Lomas said. '*Before I go hence and be no more seen.*'

'The psalmist was a wise man,' I told him, 'but he doesn't get either you or me out of our present predicament. You won't be going hence for a while yet, and as to your being no more seen, I must reserve my opinion about that for the time being.'

I must confess that as we sat there, I had few other thoughts than that Lomas was my man. I did not think the case was going to call for much detection. It would be a question of classifying facts that were fairly readily available and knocking them into some sort of order for prosecuting counsel. The time had come to have Lomas concentrating his mind.

'You know your bible pretty well,' I said.

'For years it was the only book I had in my kit-bag.'

'You didn't enjoy your army service?'

'Given my time over again, I wouldn't opt that way. I don't know that any man in his senses would.'

'You knew Gilbert Slack in the army?'

'From the start.'

'Under his thumb, were you?'

I asked it sharply. I was working almost completely in the dark. I had little information beyond the constable's notes, so my only hope was to try to get the leading suspect to tell it all. I did not much care what we talked about at first. One thing would lead to another.

'No. That's not true. I was not under his thumb. I was a corporal and he was a private. There was one time at least when I made that count.'

I was on the right lines. I could see that he was biting the bait, looking already outside his present distress and confusion.

'It is true that it was Gilbert who persuaded me to join, and took me under his wing in my recruit days.

114

And Gilbert's a rogue, I know – but he isn't a *bad* man. I've been glad in my time of Gilbert's company and help. And he of mine.'

He had been closeted all night in the fearful stench and mess of that cottage. It is true that a corpse and a broken wall cannot harm a man, but Lomas was in a highly emotional state. I did not know whether, or how much, he had been able to sleep. From the look of him, not at all. Yet here he was, beginning to talk as he might have talked at any time. It is remarkable what resources a man can sometimes find in himself. I had to keep him going, to have him making explanations – to me and to himself – until, if such were the case, he unwarily played self-condemnation into my hands. I make no attempt to defend the morality of interrogation. It is not always, not even usually, a question of bullying. The trick is, more often, to offer a much needed friendship. Whether he was a murderer or not, Lomas was in desperate need to talk to someone – and talk, and talk. All I had to do was listen – in the hope of becoming his confessor.

'You've probably never been down the coal-face,' he said.

'I have, actually. When I first joined the force I was stationed in the east of the county. Sometimes my work took me down in the cage.'

'You'll have some idea, then. Some idea, even as a visitor. The dark, the heat, the wet, the walls hemming you in.'

'Some idea,' I said sententiously.

'And I was cack-handed into the bargain. Whatever I touched went wrong. I was the laughing-stock even of my own family – only it went further than a joke. They'd never have trusted me on a shift where the real money was. Not that there was ever very much in it, but I was always employed on the mugs' jobs. By the time I was rising twenty, I was still only throwing points on the tub railway. Do you know what that means?'

'I have a rough idea.'

Lomas shifted his bottom on the broken stone wheel.

'There was a line of wagons, travelling empty to the face, then brought back loaded to the winding-shaft, pulled by an endless cable from which they could be unhooked. Ours was a skinflint pit, and over one stretch, to save boring, they ran for thirty yards through a single-line tunnel. Two cables, moving either way, passed over trunnions down the middle. The hooks on the cable were spaced for safety – provided the lads on the points didn't make mistakes. If they did, there was a derail-ment, a pile-up in the tunnel, a jammed cable, deliveries from the face stopped and a piece-work shift losing money. To say nothing of the life and limb of two points-men.'

Lomas's mind was far from Dead-Nettle now.

'I had the top end, with loaded wagons coming down to me, and at the bottom was Neddy Wardle, who was barely right in his head. It was always considered a job for someone who wasn't up to much else. All you had to do was keep your mind on what you were doing. If you hadn't it in you to think of anything else, so much the better. It was a matter of listening. Sometimes four or five hooks in a row would go by you empty, and you could leave the points across, but as soon as you heard a truck coming, you had to see that they were set to let it through. It was a miserable job; one of the wettest reaches in the pit, only your lamp for company, and if you wanted to piss even, it had to be with one hand on the lever. I'd done an eleven-hour day on that for six years.'

He was unaware now of our present surroundings.

The pale blue sky of the spring morning over Dead-Nettle meant nothing to him.

'As often as not I had to think for Neddy Wardle as well as myself. I was expected to. We couldn't see each other. We could barely make our voices heard down that tunnel. But I had to keep my ears strained for what was happening at Neddy's end, and many's the time I've saved a catastrophe by yelling to him in the nick of time to push his lever over. I felt sometimes as if I were using every ounce of the will-power I had, to keep Neddy Wardle from wrecking that cable-way.'

He wiped his forehead with the back of his hand.

'The last day – *my* last day – my mind had wandered. I'd sent a full truck down before I realised that Neddy hadn't swung over to receive it. That was his mistake, not mine, but if anything ever went wrong, I always took the blame. There was a crash, a pile-up of wrecked wagons before the cable could be stopped. The tunnel was blocked with spilled coal. They told me at the pit-head that I was under suspension whilst the deputies went into what had happened. My one thought was to get clear of the gates before my father and my brothers came up from the face – before I could run into any of my cousins, or my cousins' in-laws. I expected to be sacked, and there wouldn't be another pit in the valley that would take me.'

A pair of rabbits came scampering from a warren within yards of us. They were not bothered by us, and I do not believe that Lomas even saw them.

'It hadn't occurred to me that I wouldn't go home sooner or later that evening. In the end, I would have to face it out. But first, I just walked. And going through the town I heard a drum-and-fife band, coming over Bolsover Hill, into the Market Place. I can't describe it to you, Mr Brunt – the rhythm, the uniforms, the marching limbs, the crunching boots, men's eyes over lean, tanned cheeks that had seen all parts of the world. The thump and roll of the drum-sticks on the donkey-skins seemed to be beating right down into me. There they were in their ceremonial reds, and there was I, big boned and weakly, pale-faced behind the coal-dust, still in my pit clothes. I marched behind the band – not marched, slouched – but in step, on the soles of my feet rather than my heels. If only I could march into battle with them! It's funny, isn't it? I didn't even think they would have me.'

There was some sort of amusement in his eyes for a moment, but it was short-lived and embittered.

'It was a small detachment: a platoon, I can tell you that now. They halted in the middle of the market cobbles, and were given the order to *Fall out*, and I, like many another, lads from the pits and the work-benches, girls from the mills and the shop counters, hung about watching them. My eye was caught by a trio of whom Gilbert Slack and Harry Burgess were a couple, and when they went stamping into the *Grapes*, I felt as if I'd lost them for ever. But I was still loitering on the pavement when they came out, hoping, I suppose, that they would fall in again, and the band would start up. And this time Gilbert caught my eye – they'd had a glass to drink but were far from drunk – and he jerked his head for me to tack on to them. We only went across the road to the *Chequers*, and I'd never been in such a place before. It was very much against Chapel, but I think I knew by then that I had to leave hearth and home for good.'

He looked at me as if begging my credence.

'They talked loudly, for the benefit of everyone in the tavern – and, of course, for free drinks. Tales of distant places – none of which, I know now, they had ever been to. They were still a home battalion. They told yarns of how they had bested their sergeants and officers. And all the while, in a sly, winking way, Gilbert Slack was making himself my friend. Half an hour later it was *A man like you ought to be one of us*. "I'd never thought," I said. "Do you reckon – ?" and then we were in a third inn, the *Hammer and Nails*, where there was a sergeant sitting at a table with a knot of civilians. Gilbert brought me to him, and he bought us more ale. And I was enlisted.'

'Slack sold you into bondage, for a quart for himself and his mates?'

'It's an honourable calling,' Lomas said earnestly. 'We have no right to call it bondage.'

'But you know what I mean.'

'I know only too well what you mean.'

I would need to know a good deal more about the love-hate between Lomas and Slack, if I was ever to understand this affair. But would I ever need to *understand* it? I went on trying to drive in the wedge.

'All the same, Slack was thinking of no one but himself.'

'People do Gilbert an injustice,' Lomas said.

I wondered what people he meant – if any. I later grasped he was thinking of Isobel Fuller.

'It was very different, coming into barracks for the first time – a very different sergeant from the fat man laughing over his tankard. I was in a lot of trouble in the army in my early days – and after. But I'd have been in even more if it hadn't been for Gilbert. He taught me more about soldiering than my sergeant ever did.'

'You mean about column-dodging?'

He managed a faint and fleeting grin. 'That, too. A man has to learn to survive. But we didn't dodge the column when the Boer lead was flying about.'

'No. And you were in Gilbert Slack's company, were you, when you met your wife?'

Frank Lomas nodded gravely, and his eyes strayed over to the uncurtained windows of the dreadful hovel. 'I'd like to tell you about that, Mr Brunt.'

'Please do.'

I was his friend. Like Gilbert Slack.

CHAPTER FIFTEEN

The battalion had mustered in Nottingham and marched in laps through the Midlands and round London to Rochester. Frank Lomas survived all his scrapes, his extra guard duties and his penal fatigues and attained the status of a trained soldier. There was an extended field exercise on the Isle of Thanet, followed by a sudden release from frayed tempers and discipline. After days of pointless standing-to in dew-drenched hedge-bottoms, there was a cleaning-up of uniforms and a relaxation of training. Officers disappeared on furlough. In warm spring sunshine men pipe-clayed equipment, furbished brass buckles and set off in twos and threes to look for uncritical hearts to charm.

That was the afternoon when Slack shocked Lomas by stealing from the counter of a village shop. They came into St Nicholas-at-Wade where the striped canvas canopies were fluttering over the booths and rounda-bouts of a fair on the green. Steam-driven wooden horses with bulging eyes and flaring nostrils; ostriches and peacocks, their plush seats crowded with laughing girls in bonnets, waving parasols. Brandy-snap, warm and sticky from the stalls; coloured paper balls on elastic, which a man was entitled, in the happiness of carnival, to bounce into the face of a laughing stranger. Gilbert Slack almost got into a fight with a man in charge of a shy, whom he accused of weighting the coconuts to their plinths with lumps of lead. The try-your-strength machine was out of commission for the rest of the day after Frank Lomas had brought down the mall on its wooden peg. There was nothing weakly about him after the months of fresh air and physical exercise.

Squeals of delight and admiration behind him, and that was when they picked up the three girls: Gilbert took Patsy, a nut-brown, shiny-cheeked nubile girl from Whitstable, whose breasts would surely burst at any moment out of her bodice; Harry took Kate, a slow moving, slow spoken Amazon even bigger than himself; Frank Lomas paired off with Hetty, surely the outstanding trophy of the three, a girl in gossamer, with the innocence and scrubbed happiness of a dairy-maid cast in Derby china.

They went off towards a wood on the edge of a water-meadow, Harry with his arm about the big girl's waist, Gilbert and Patsy so closely entwined that it was a wonder they could walk at all. Frank Lomas held Hetty Wilson's hand. He was surprised that she did not repel him. Hitherto his sole aspirations had been hopeless day-dreams about a chapel choir-girl on whom he had gazed over the brilliantined heads of respectable miners on Sunday nights.

He worshipped Hetty Wilson from the moment that their eyes met. The miracle to him was that she seemed content to eschew other company that afternoon for his. He did not, of course, tell me all that they talked

about as they strolled down that lane, its banks a float-
ing vapour of bluebells. I dare say he could have remembered it in affectionate detail – and I am sure that it
was as proper as anything he could have found to say
to his choir-girl. I am equally sure that Hetty Wilson –
at first, at any rate – must have been fascinated by him.
She laughed gaily at some of the things he said, sometimes with the sharp, cynical wit of a town girl, but
never unkindly, for she saw how seriously he seemed
to take life. It seems obvious to me that Frank Lomas
was a challenge to Hetty Wilson from the start. He
must at the time have been in the prime of a superb
physique. He was a good looking man, probably with a
good deal of the overgrown boy still in his features.
He was clean shaven – and, of course, not yet lame.
Most of all, consciously or otherwise, it was his integrity
that enticed her. It was something she had to over-
power. I know the likes of Hetty Wilson. When Frank
Lomas talked about her, he gave her away more vividly
than he understood her himself.

Once in the wood, the three couples went separate
ways. Harry and Kate sank down in a hollow on the
river bank. Gilbert and Patsy disappeared behind an
alder-bush over which Gilbert's scarlet tunic was
presently thrown unceremoniously, its buttons glinting
haphazardly in the sun. Frank Lomas led Hetty some
distance away from the others, towards a hummock
overlooking a bend of brook that was embraced by an
arc of pollarded willows. Turning over his shoulder he
caught a glimpse of Gilbert Slack, his trousers loose
about the knees, his pink buttocks wriggling as Patsy
lay under him, her legs splayed out on either side of
his in wooden surrender.

Lomas's desire was to steer Hetty past the place
before she could catch sight of what was going on, but

she seemed to know better than to look. He led her round to the opposite rim of the rise.

'Are we going to sit up here, then?' she asked him.

They commanded a view of the close hedgerows of the Kentish countryside, the steeples of the church behind a shimmering haze, the bunting and pavilions of the fairground, a stream of couples strung out between the green and its perimeter of orchards and meadows.

'It'll be more fun down there – more *private*.'

She skipped down the slope ahead of him, whilst he followed in his parade-ground boots, catching a sudden objective image of himself as something of an oaf on whom this sudden fortune had inexplicably descended. There can be no doubt that Hetty was the picture of delicate femininity, her skirts of heliotrope chiffon rustling against the pollened grass, as if herself a personification of the lady's-smocks with which the terrain was strewn.

She led him along the water's edge to an overgrown bank which had already been pressed into a receptive bed by other shoulders.

'No – not there. Let's make a corner of our own,' she said, and he was ashamed of himself for having implied that another man's left-over palette was good enough for her.

She lowered herself to the ground and sat back on her elbows with her knees raised. He dropped self-consciously beside her, was shy of initiating physical contact, though they were so close that he was aware of the warmth of her body. For minutes they sat thus, in desultory conversation, commanded by the bowl of blue sky with its fleecy clouds, the water breasting reeds a few yards away from them, a cuckoo calling from a copse on the further bank. A blue and green dragonfly hovered over them, as if on a visit of inspection. She gave a little squeal, mistaking it for a stinging insect. Two hands waved to ward it off: his huge and weathered, hers slender and pale. Flesh touched flesh and his fingers closed over hers.

She leaned her head back against the greenery and looked up into his face, blue eyes titillating him with friendly impudence. At the same time, she lowered her knees and brought up her limbs alongside his. He plunged then, bent his chest over her with his hand under her shoulders and kissed her with an immense release of fervour. A minute later she pushed him away, not in complaint, but with gasping laughter, coming up for air. She adjusted her position, put her hands about his cheeks with her fingers in his hair and brought down his face for her to kiss, now with full lips. He drew himself down to the length of her, marvelled at the softness of her breasts and the warmth of her secret places. He felt then the committal flush of his whole body, the sum of his instincts surging for release. A short while later it was he who had to break away, turn partially from her, edge himself back, but even then too late to prevent a private catastrophe. He thanked God that she could not know what was happening to him. And he was desperately afraid that she might misunderstand his apparent rejection of her. But she smiled at him like a kind of conspirator.

'It's a long time, isn't it, since you were out with anyone like me?'

He did not tell her that it was the first and only time.

'You need to calm yourself down a bit.'

And how little, he thought, she knew the truth of her words. If love was blind, in Frank Lomas's case it was also gratuitously swathed in the bindings of the years. They remained for a long time on that river bank, talking. When they got up to go back to the village, to look for something to eat and drink at one of the fairground stalls, the two other couples were not to be found. Lomas was concerned about them.

'Good heavens!' Hetty said. 'They're big enough to look after themselves, I should think. And we don't need *them*, do we?'

In the next few days, in the wave of slackness and leisure that seemed to have descended on the regiment, they saw a great deal of each other. Hetty appeared to have no more calls on her time. She told him that she was not from this district, but from a village in Hampshire, and was holidaying with relatives on Minster Marshes. They trespassed over farm-fields and paddocks, and one day she took him to a lonely shed where, on a hay-pile, with the smell of dry chaff and old sacking in his nostrils, he made love to her for the first time.

It was rapidly, one might say brutally, broached and soon over. But she seemed to accept this philosophically and was not woebegone in her disappointment.

'And now that you've got that out of your system,' she said, 'it's time that you learned a few things.'

'Learned a few things?'

'Learned to take your time. Be strong, Frank – be as strong as you like. But you've got to learn to be gentle at the same time. Love is a gentle thing. I'm only a little girl, remember. Not a sack strung up on a frame for bayonet practice.'

'I'm sorry.'

'Don't be sorry, Frank. It was nice. Only it could be nicer.'

It is amazing that he did not see through her then, that he had not seen through her already. But men can have a remarkable obstinacy in not believing what they do not want to believe. And in Frank Lomas's case, his purblindness was cluttered up under a huddle of additional blinkers. It must surely have occurred to him that Hetty Wilson was not inexperienced. But perhaps he thought he was to be the last of her adventures. Perhaps he was overwhelmed by the single-mindedness with which she wanted him. And this was no delusion. She did want him. She had wanted him savagely on that first sight of him on the fairground. I do not doubt his virility, and I expect that as he became accustomed to intimate contact with her, he arrived at a better command of his timing. Moreover, she found him an attractively curious man; she had never met anyone like him. Even his manner of speech added piquancy to their walks.

The upshot of it was that he wanted to marry her. It was not that he was beginning to be filled already with puritanical remorse. The life he was leading with her was too vital for that, too elemental – and too continuous. But he was unable to distinguish between love and physical impulse, and love and marriage simply were not separate entities in his ethical background.

She ran the whole range of conventional ways of putting him off; naïve shock and surprise at his declamation; a plea for thinking time; a spate of self-denigration that he mistook for a charming trick to make him flood her with denials.

'But you don't know me, Frank. You don't know what a horrible woman I am, under the surface.'

'There's nothing horrible about you.'

'You don't know some of the things I have done in my time.'

Beyond the need she felt to discourage him, I think she had developed a definite affection for him – of a sort.

'I don't care about anything that happened in the past,' he said.

How suicidal can a man become?

'No, Frank – I'm not for you. Let's enjoy what we've had. Let's go on enjoying it while we can. But let's not kid ourselves about the future.'

But it was beyond his character to adopt such an attitude. Then, unaccountably, she changed her mind.

Unaccountably: even when he talked to me about it, on the crumbling remains of the Dead-Nettle crushing-wheel, the poor devil still did not know what it was all about. He had never been able to read the clues, though it had struck him at the time as difficult to understand how so much of his private affairs seemed to be general knowledge in the platoon lines.

'What's all this about wanting to get married?' Gilbert Slack had asked him.

'Who told you about that?'

'Hetty told Patsy. And you must be a bloody idiot, Frank. You need to get hold of yourself. Find 'em, fool 'em and forget 'em, that's my motto. Whip it in, whip it out and wipe it.'

'That's not my way of looking at things.'

'But what do you think you're ever going to do with her, Frank? You've another six years' colour service still to get in.'

'That's not a life-time, Gilbert. She'll wait.'

'You think so?'

'She wouldn't have me anyway,' Frank said, paradoxically.

'You never want to go by a woman's first answer,' Gilbert told him. 'I happen to know that you've bowled her off her feet. And she was supposed to be a hard nut to crack.'

'Where did you get that from?'

'From Patsy.'

The next evening, Hetty changed her mind. To Frank

Lomas it was a sacred moment. Though bubblingly happy about it, Hetty did not behave as if she had radically reversed a decision. It was almost as if, on an impulse, she had turned in to buy a new hat that she had been looking at for days in a shop window.

They made an appointment with the vicar. Neither of them was on the parish roll, but within the compass of the law, the church counted – or could be made to count, if the priest-in-charge was willing – as Hetty's normal place of worship. It might easily have gone the other way, but a certain latitude was adopted to accommodate a passing soldier.

The second time the banns were read, the battalion was on Sunday parade in the village church. It seemed as if every neck, from the Adjutant to the youngest bugler, was twisted towards Lomas when his name was announced.

On the Tuesday after that week-end there was an infusion of new activity in their camp. Several officers returned from furlough. There was an issue of tropical kit from the Quartermaster's store. Lomas's platoon sergeant stood before them with a new joy in his animal eyes.

'Say goodbye to your sweethearts and wives.'

The regiment was confined to camp pending overseas draft. Lomas knew nothing that he could do about it. He did not think of asking his company officer to intercede for a special licence for them. He did not know enough about the marriage laws. And in any case, his was not that kind of company officer. He would have had to wait forty-eight hours even to speak to him, having submitted a written request through the sergeant.

Then suddenly the padre waylaid him on a wagon scrubbing fatigue.

'What's all this about you getting married, and the third banns not called, Private Lomas?'

Apparently the chaplain had heard it all from the vicar, and demanded now to hear it all again from Frank.

'And is she – ? Is the young lady – ?'

He looked meaningfully at Frank. Frank blushed. It was a possibility that had occurred to him.

'Well, we shall have to do something about it, then, shan't we? We shall have to see if the Bishop, in the circumstances, will grant us his licence. And I'll have to ask the Colonel if we can marry you on a special church parade. It would do us all good, I am sure, at a time like this, to show a little military swagger.'

And that was how it was carried out. The Colonel entered into the spirit of it as if it were the very thing that his regiment's morale needed on the eve of embarkation. The battalion fell in in hollow square under command of the Regimental Sergeant-Major, the Corps of Drums leading. Lomas's platoon applied themselves to a man to the dressing and polishing of him. They stood him on a sheet of newspaper, as they did with men detailed for guard, so that he should not damage the shine on the studs of his boots before the moment of the ceremony. The grossness of the men's conversation knew no limits.

He was not allowed to see Hetty before they marched him out to the parade square. It was said to be unlucky. He had not set eyes on her since before the news of their departure had been announced. She appeared to have been entertained in the officers' mess on the wedding morning, and was actually given away by the Senior Subaltern. Fortunately neither Lomas nor any of his mates knew of the concept of *droit de seigneur*. They seemed to have plied her, too, with a good deal to drink. And indeed, most of the lieutenants on parade were in similar case. Lomas had no chance to exchange any talk with her at all as the padre intoned the service. But her speech was almost too slurred for her to repeat the necessary phrases after him, and Lomas desperately wanted to help her out with them.

An undisciplined cheer went up from a thousand right-dressed men when he kissed her, under the padre's orders. Then they were led by a drummer to a single bell-tent that had been pitched at an extremity of the compound. Lomas was made to lift her in his arms and carry her under the flap. An orderly then lashed up the canvas from outside and a bugler sounded *No Parade*. The battalion certainly appears to have enjoyed itself that day.

Hetty fell asleep – or into a stupor – the moment he laid her on the bed. She was still in a virtual coma the next morning when he had to leave her. It had been a long night, a lonely and dark one under canvas (by oversight or intention no lamp had been provided for them). He stroked Hetty's sweating brow for an hour at a time, but was unable to establish any communication with her.

The next morning, a runner called Lomas early. It was as if the army, to round off the verve with which it had risen to the emergency, had also judged it fit to operate a *came the dawn* reminder. Lomas's fun was over. So was everyone else's. He was at work before general Reveille, one of the baggage party, forming a chain of stores to wagons for the first stage of their journey to the Cape.

There were women with handkerchiefs held to their reddened eyes on the platform of Sturry Station as the band from the Depot played *Auld Lang Syne* to the departing train. But Hetty Lomas was not up and about in time to be amongst them. It was more than seven years before Lomas was to see her again, walking up to meet him in a Derby street, with Duncan Mottershead waiting as potential master of ceremonies in a darkened archway.

On the troop-ship, and from camps all over South Africa, he had written to her at the address in Kent which he believed to be hers, but there came no reply. He asked the padre to have enquiries made, and this the padre promised him would be done. But he continued without news and was not convinced that behind the scenes and across the oceans any man was bothering on his behalf.

When he was finally discharged from military hospital, he made his way again to St Nicholas-at-Wade, where he failed signally to compose a working description of her. Try as he may, he could find no trace. Nor could he get anyone to remember Gilbert Slack's Patsy or Harry Burgess's Kate.

'Of course,' someone said in the *Bell*. 'When all those troops were formed up here to wait their turn for Southampton, there was a whole pack of girls came in from Aldershot.'

Then he caught sight of Frank Lomas's brow and his dangling hand, and he hastened to add, 'But she wouldn't have been one of those.'

Aldershot: *a village in Hampshire?*

She'd said that, hadn't she, speaking perhaps with some measure of truth.

CHAPTER SIXTEEN

He came to Margreave and Dead-Nettle, pitted himself
against the mother rock, made friends with Isobel
Fuller. Then suddenly a letter came for him. How could
his wife possibly have discovered his whereabouts? It
could only have been through Gilbert Slack. No doubt
he was still in touch with regimental friends, and one
or other of them, by some chance, with Hetty.

It was a pathetically silly letter. She must have pinned
child-like faith in his credulity; and not in vain – she
got him to Derby.

She had lost, she said, the little diary in which she
had noted his regimental address. She had written to him
many letters, with many tentative designations. They
must have all gone astray. She had even applied to the
War Office, who had sent her no reply. It had all been
hopeless.

*And of course what has made it so much worse is
that you are not the only Frank Lomas now. You
wouldn't have wanted me to call him anything but
Frank, would you, my darling?*

He did not believe a word that she said in the first
part of the letter. Her transparent falsity sickened him.
But this talk of the birth of a son called out – as it was
meant to – to every last nuance of his plodding old
sense of duty. He had to go to Derby, and wrote to her
at the address she now gave him – Emma Rice's boarding-house. He gave her a date and a time.

And he had to bring her back from Derby to Margreave even though, in the moment he recognised her
coming up that street, he saw her for exactly what she

was. These were the eyes into which he had looked on the river bank at St Nicholas, the cheeky eyes that had taught him how to make love to her own satisfaction, the clouded eyes that had not known where she was, when she had stood at his side on the church parade.

And he must have been making comparisons now with Isobel Fuller.

He brought Hetty back to Dead-Nettle. She said that she had left their son with a cousin. In Hampshire. It could possibly be true. So Lomas would stand by the pair of them, even though by now he hated her with a hatred that defied expression, a hatred which he frankly confessed to me. Was it a hatred strong enough for him to have killed her?

I have said that at the outset he was my man. My certainty had weakened as he unfolded his tale of naïve integrity and rough-hearted tenderness. But now, as he owned to his hatred, I knew that my sympathy might now – and at any moment – have to defer to my duty.

Had he hated her, more than anything else, for the damage she had wrought between him and Isobel? Might she, in the end, have lost her temper and jeered at him, lashed out and boastfully revealed the tawdry arts with which she had manipulated him, that far off fair-day in Kent? Would she, as a woman of her kind, have sought to put back the clock by enticing him to make love to her again in that lead-miner's shack? And might he not, after such an encounter, have turned against her in counter-revulsion? Was there such a clear-cut dividing line between animal sex and animal murder?

There was a tale that had gone round the village, P.C. Newton had included it in his notes: Hetty Lomas's scream that had riven the countryside, the first night she was here. Had that been an intimation of violence to come?

133

I asked Lomas bluntly about it. He remembered it as if it were something from an existence already forgotten.

'I can tell you about that,' he said.

'I'm asking you.'

'She screamed because she saw me take off my trousers.'

I forbore to say that her outlook on life must have undergone a remarkable change.

'She saw me take off my trousers and she caught sight of my leg – my wound, the twisted muscle that's left of it, my distorted foot. I know it's pretty horrible. I can imagine the sight of it turning anyone sick. I wouldn't have thought, though, that it would make a woman scream out into the night.'

'That depends on the woman.'

'It's funny, because – '

'What's funny about it?'

'Oh, nothing.'

I did not know at that moment of Isobel's reaction to the same wound. I let the subject go now. I did not want to be side-tracked.

Had Frank Lomas simply come home unexpectedly early from Chapel to find her in the act of pulling down his wall, looking for Gilbert Slack's plunder in his home? Had Slack offered her a sizeable share, in exchange for retrieving it for him? Had she and Slack been in league with each other ever since that spring in Kent? And if Lomas had come to a sudden realisation of that, even the suspicion of it, would there have been any stopping him? Hadn't violence crossed his mind, even in that moment of understanding in the Derby street?

Lomas was no fool – at bottom. He read my mind, if not in detail, at least in outline. Not for the first time while we had been talking together, his eyes strayed in the direction of the cottage.

'I didn't kill her,' he said, for the first time, with a simplicity that many men would have found telling, but against which I schooled myself.

'No?'

'No. But I did kill a woman once. It's not a thing that brings me any pride, and it's not a thing that a man could do twice.'

He wanted me to ask him to go on, but I allowed a short silence to increase the tension. Somewhere a crow shrieked, driving a marauder away from his private carrion. In the distance we heard the crump of blasting in one of the quarries.

'That reminds me of the very time,' Lomas said.

'Tell me about it.'

It had been in the later stages of the war. There had been a sudden desperate strait, an unexpected flush of casualties. The order had been cooks, officers' servants, even sanitary corporals in the ranks. Lomas's platoon had been sent out on a forward patrol, to try to engage and pin down a ranging troop of Boer horsemen. His lieutenant and sergeant had both been killed. The command of the patrol had devolved on him, but the men – Slack amongst them – had started their own council of war about what to do next. They were for pressing back the way they had come. No one took Frank Lomas's honourable stripes seriously.

Yet he suddenly entrenched himself and stood firm on his authority. He could see that the only sane thing to do was to go to earth before twilight and try to regain the battalion at dawn. He threatened to lay charges, on their return, against any man who was insubordinate.

'Including you,' he said to Slack.

'Don't be an imbecile, Frank.'

'Try me out, then.'

'It's funny, Mr Brunt. They didn't have to do what I

said. If they'd stuck together and defied me, I'd have had no evidence against them. I'd nothing on my side bar the tone of my voice.'

Which showed me again that Lomas was no dummy. He could rise to occasions – when he was moved. It was a pity it had always taken so much to stir him.

He put down the patrol under cover on the outskirts of a farmstead that appeared to be deserted – a likely possibility, since the men-folk were probably out skirmishing, and the women all gathered in a central corral elsewhere. He drew up a watch-roster for the coming night. And he allowed Gilbert Slack to go foraging. That was a reasonable proposition: their own supplies were thin, and Slack was a good provider. He made his way over to the farm and was a long time gone. They saw him coming back across a yard carrying a crate of what looked like home-made wine. From the nature of his progress, it was obvious that he had already assured himself of its potency.

Lomas lay looking over his cover when a shot was fired and a bullet chipped stone only inches from Slack's foot. Lomas saw a woman with a Mauser at her shoulder, taking fresh aim through the upper half of a stable door.

She was middle-aged, matronly in a fleshless way and had been blonde in her youth, though her hair was now the colour of dirty straw and pulled tightly across her head from a central parting. Someone called out – uselessly – to warn Gilbert. Lomas steadied his foresight over the woman's left breast, clasped the cold stock of his Lee Enfield against his cheek and took first pressure on the trigger. It seemed an age before he could summon up the nerve to fire his bullet. Seconds elapsed like taut empty hours. Then he squeezed his forefinger.

'Me, Mr Brunt. I killed her. Can you look at me now, knowing anything about me at all, even what little bit you've found out in the last few minutes, and believe that I'd do a thing like that?'

I thought of no ready answer. That he'd done it to defend a friend? It wasn't the first story I'd heard in which the true horror of war had been something apart from the main issue. Lomas spoke again before I could.

'I saw the jerk of her body as the bullet hit her. A working woman, the mother of a family, a grandmother too, probably, firing at an intruder who was robbing her larder. I saw that look come into her eyes: the shock, and then the final, clear understanding. I must have hit her somewhere vital: the main artery below the heart, I think. She dropped her rifle and died within seconds – but they were long seconds, seconds in which she knew she was going to die, just as for long seconds I had known I was going to kill her. The look on her face has been with me ever since.'

Gilbert Slack had scrambled back amongst them, dragging his crate of Transvaal hock, shrill and hilarious; hysterical almost, with delayed fear, secondary shock – and the amount he had already drunk. He swore eternal brotherhood with Frank Lomas.

'And if they ride back and find us here with her body,' Lomas told them, 'they will hang us all from that tree – *after* a few preliminaries.'

He doubled the guard. It was that night, maudlin and excitable, that Slack told him about Dead-Nettle.

'The man who fills his dish in that mine, Frank, will drive his pick into a fortune. I'm telling you this, because you are my friend. There isn't another living soul in the whole wide world that I would tell it to.'

'That look on the Dutch woman's face,' I said to Lomas. 'Describe it to me again.'

He looked at me surprised. I insisted that he try to repeat his description. The second time, in cold blood,

it was almost perfunctory. But I did not disbelieve either
the experience or the intensity of his memory.

'Now tell me about the look on Hetty's face,' I told
him, 'when she saw you were going to kill her.'

CHAPTER SEVENTEEN

It did not work. I could not shock or confuse Lomas
into unintentional admissions. My attempt to bully
him succeeded only in destroying the rapport that had
begun to grow between us. The chance to talk to me
had done something for him. When I stirred up his
distrust, he looked hurt. As I walked away from the
mine, I knew I had done badly. It would be hard work
getting our relationship back to the point where it had
started.

But I could not afford to become sentimental about
Frank Lomas merely because I was tempted to like him.
Reason still made him the most likely culprit, but there
was nothing yet on which I felt justified in holding
him. Why had he left Chapel before the end of the
service? Where had he gone then and why? How came
he to have blood on his boots? Why had he gone off wandering into the hills again after finding his wife's body?
His answers to those questions were artless enough to
tempt belief. He had found the sermon offensive to his
present condition. He had wanted solitude and physical
movement to allow himself to think. When he had seen
the violence that had been done at Dead-Nettle, his

instinct had been to range out looking for the marauder. He was well out into the night before he realised what a purposeless chase he was on. His was not an impressive story : if it was untrue, then it was a feeble effort indeed. For that reason alone, I could not reject it out of hand. He had apparently not thought it necessary to think very hard in terms of self-exoneration.

I had asked him what his immediate plans were and he had freely admitted that he was giving up the search for ore. Come the warmer weather, he would be on the move : but he did not want town life. Perhaps one of the pits in his home region might give him a surface job. He was a lost man, played out, thinking in vague terms of a return to the coal-field because his imagination as well as his grit seemed to have deserted him.

I had not the resources even to keep him under adequate surveillance. I had one sergeant and one detective-constable with me, and a message to Derby asking for reinforcements was not likely to produce miracles. I set D.C. Fordyce to keep unobtrusive watch on the mine, but this was not a vigil that could be kept up round the clock. In the course of the day the interim report reached me that after mooning about on his slag-heap, Lomas had suddenly taken to clearing up in the cottage. He brought out rubble and filth, scrubbed his matting and began to dig over the earth floor where the body had lain. None of this suggested a man about to take flight.

I went to Margreave Hall and talked first to Isobel Fuller, thinking to find her an intelligent if not placid subject. I found her attractive – a mature and bonny woman, if one looked past her immediate fatigue and distress. But it was apparent that she had been badly shaken. I do not mean that there was any marked lack of self-control. It would not be going too far to describe her for the most part as poised : a woman trained and inclined to deal with current situations and not pander to herself. Her upset took the form of a somewhat distant, almost cynical attitude to unpalatable facts.

'Are you coming to arrest me?'

'Do you think I ought to?'

I could have gone on then to press her for her reasons why I should suspect her. I preferred to sit and look at her in silence for prolonged seconds, then ask her the plain and obvious questions. She had gone to meet Lomas outside his chapel, she said. There had been things she had wanted to discuss with him. There were aspects of his personal conduct on which she felt he owed her an explanation.

'It was on the spur of the moment, you understand, Inspector. Arrogant of me. He owes me nothing. He is a married man, and that is the sum total of it.'

'*Was* a married man, Miss Fuller.'

She looked sharply at me. 'Implying?'

'Getting our tenses right. No implication. Frank Lomas usually went to Chapel, did he?'

'Usually, to the best of my knowledge. I am not responsible for Mr Lomas's movements, Inspector.'

'Oh, come, Miss Fuller. You knew where to go to meet him.'

'Sorry. Yes, I did.'

'But you weren't in the habit of going to Chapel with him?'

She laughed, drily and briefly. 'I don't – didn't – share his views, Inspector. Merely respected them.'

'Now it is you who are speaking in the past tense. Of a man who is still alive.'

'A manner of speaking. What does it matter what tense I use?'

'It might suggest a change of attitude towards the man.'

'None whatsoever.'

I find that with normally intelligent people who are being unreasonable under distress, silence is often more effective than vituperation. I sat looking uncomfortable and said nothing.

'I'm sorry, Inspector. I'm tired.'

'And not quite sure of your own mind.'

I said this as gently as I could. I was not being provocative. She looked the type who would presently settle down and co-operate.

'Of course, you are right,' she said, having herself used a moment of silence instead of rhetoric. 'And dangerously near to stepping outside the limits of your duty.'

'My duty has no limits – in a case like this.'

She looked at me more keenly. 'You mean that your mind wasn't made up about the murderer, the moment you heard the facts of the case?'

'Should it have been?'

'You know what I mean. Please don't try to put words into my mouth.'

'It is enough for me to know that you have them on your mind.'

'What's on my mind – or what you think is on my mind – is hardly evidence, is it, Mr Brunt?'

'Not evidence at all. But it might help me on my way to the truth – which is what interests me. You too, I I hope.'

'I'm not sure.'

'I would have thought – '

'As a policeman, it has become part of your second nature to ferret out facts. I'm not sure that the truth will do anyone any good.'

'Not even if it clears those unjustly suspected?'

'That, yes. I suppose I must be one of your suspects too. I dare say I can live with the thought.'

'Do you think that Frank Lomas could have killed his wife?'

'I'd rather not answer that.'

'Thank you. You have answered it.'

'Let us not play dramatic games, Inspector. Most of the men who have known Hetty Lomas, and any man married to her, must surely have come near to murder on occasion.'

'You knew her well personally, I take it?'

'I talked to her for five minutes, the day before yesterday, when I went to collect the rent.'

'So you are accustomed to making confident judgements? You heard a lot about her from Lomas perhaps?'

'Never a word. That is what –'

'Rankles?'

'That is what I wanted to see him about on Sunday evening. Or should I say half wanted to. I was more than half relieved when he was not there.'

'You were going to take him to task, because he had not told you about his wife?'

'Not take to task – well, yes – take to task.'

'You considered him under that kind of obligation to you?'

'Not an obligation, Inspector. But in the nature of the relationship between us –'

She stopped. What she had been about to say needed better wording.

'How would you summarise that relationship, Miss Fuller?'

'We were friends.'

'Yes.'

And when I saw her anger gathering, I added, 'I am

not saying *yes* satirically. I accept what you say. Why shouldn't I ?'

'Mr Brunt, I laughed just now, when you asked if I used to go to Chapel with Frank. That would have given Margreave some complex satisfaction. My God, I wish now I had.'

She closed her eyes, partly from weariness, partly to help herself to think.

'I expect you'll have heard – I expect people met your train to tell you on the platform – that I once spent a whole night at Dead-Nettle – that being, in the circumstances, the only balanced and sensible thing to do. What is so outrageous in a night spent in a cottage ? If we had wanted to comport ourselves as everyone assumes we did, what would have been wrong with half past ten in the morning ? Inspector, I wish you could have seen how Frank behaved that night. It would have been laughable, if it hadn't been so genuine. His modesty and prudence were out of this world. He went out of his way at the beginning to tell me I had nothing to fear. To *fear*! He gave me his bed and slept somehow himself downstairs. He wouldn't even come up into the second bedroom. And he went out into the stable while I undressed, wouldn't come into the house again until he saw that my candle was out.'

Later, before I left Margreave, Lomas was to pour out his heart to me about this and many other things. He told me how he had gone out into the snow that night while she got ready for bed. But it had not been her modesty that he was protecting. It was himself; he wanted her so badly. And for a long time after going back into the cottage he lay awake wrestling with tension – with the temptation to go up the ladder, to make a noise, to wake her, to have her to talk to him in the hope that that might lead them together. He resisted – partly because he could not bear to associate Isobel with the way he had made love to Hetty.

Later on, after Christmas, they did make love. He told me that simply, and without embroidery. I formed the impression that they moved towards the act together, perhaps after a chance physical contact. It happened more than once; regularly, I presume, in February and March. But they had not so far made any permanent plans, though they both knew that the necessity to do so hung over them. They were loving each other out of natural necessity, there being some vague point ahead of them, the end of the winter, when they knew they would have to face up to practicalities.

I learned, of course, none of this from Isobel Fuller herself. I would not have expected to.

'We were good friends,' she said. 'Very good friends indeed. I will not try to hide the fact of the matter from you, Inspector: if he would have considered marrying me, I would have taken him with joy. But I had to wait patiently for him to see his way through problems that afflicted him alone. And my God, I know now, what those problems were. I had a future all mapped out for us.'

'And may I ask what it was?'

'Margreave Hall will be mine when my father dies. The sooner we can get rid of Slack and Burgess, the better. Then Frank can come in from the mine and take charge of the work they are playing with. He can start learning to manage the estate. It is a job he could do to perfection. Ultimately, then, he could be its master.'

'You hadn't mentioned this to him?'

'You do not know Frank. To present such a plan to him prematurely would be fatal. He might even have upped sticks in a gallant bid to save me from myself.

That's just how he would probably have put it : a natural candidate for the Round Table.'

'There may be time for you yet,' I said.

She lowered her eyelids. 'Don't, Inspector. Don't try to work things out for us.'

As I have mentioned, she knew by this time that she was pregnant by Lomas, but she did not tell me this; simply continued with her rationalisations; the truth, but only part of it.

'Can't you see now why I felt bitter? Why I was relieved to escape that Sunday evening? Why I was only half anxious to confront him? Why I believe that I had the right to know that he was a married man? When I first heard that she had come, my fury was unbounded. I made an excuse to go round and see her; malicious curiosity, as much as anything else. And I'm glad I did. It helped me to get her and Frank into focus. I knew then that Frank was free from blame – except perhaps for sheer stupidity. He hadn't done much wrong in my book for having tried to forget a woman like that. But where had she been all these years? Had he ever gone into the legal aspects of her having deserted him? Had he messed up his chances of a divorce by having her back to live with him? He is the sort of man who will accept as his natural lot a misfortune of any magnitude. That's one of the things that rankles with me most : the fact that he never trusted himself to discuss any of this with me at all. We might have found a way out of his problems together.'

'And all this is what you'd have talked about on Sunday evening?'

'I'd have seen how things went. I'd have brought things out into the open, at least.'

'Instead of which, when he wasn't in Chapel – ?'

'I went for a walk in the dark – to try to think things

out more clearly. To try also to stay out until my father had gone to bed. He was on the verge of asking questions.'

'You didn't think of going to visit the Lomases at home?'

'No.'

'That had never occurred to you?'

'It had occurred to me. I'm ashamed to say that I shirked it.'

'So which way did you go?'

'Up Ranters' Hill by Thorn Farm.'

'What were you wearing?'

She looked at me with surprise and some apprehension – even more so when I wrote down a list of the items in my book. It was the first thing she had said that I had noted down.

'And where are those things now?'

She shrugged her shoulders. 'Put aside for the wash, mainly. It was a muddy night. I got pretty filthy.'

'If I could examine those things, Miss Fuller – now, if you please. They might be a useful source of elimination.'

She sighed.

My interviews today seemed to be following a melancholy pattern. They tended to end on a note that destroyed the confidence that I had been at such pains to build up.

CHAPTER EIGHTEEN

She led me up by the back stairs. I took it that this was simply a short cut. There was no social artificiality about the Fullers. We came to a bedroom corridor on which a servant was putting soiled linen into a bolster-case. Esmond Fuller kept, according to the standards of the time – and especially in view of the image which he had originally come to Margreave to display – a relatively modest establishment. Consequently Isobel controlled the work of the household with some knowledge of its detail. In the few words which she exchanged with this elderly woman, for example, she showed that she knew the peculiarities of individual sheets.

'Wash-day tomorrow. A woman comes in Tuesdays early. So you're here on the right day.'

She took me into a dressing-room, now used as a sort of clearing-house, and pointed to yesterday's clothes on a pile. There was certainly mud in profuse evidence. A damp stain had gone through a frock and carried blue dye to her underskirt. A cashmere stocking had been torn by a thorn. Thanks to the developments of forensic science, I could doubtless have provided a merry old time for our under-manned county laboratory with brushings of dust. I did not think that it was worth taking samples for analysis, just to show she had been where we knew she had. It was blood that I was looking for. The absence of it would prove nothing to us; its presence would be highly suggestive. There were a few specks where the thorn had torn the stocking, nothing more.

I have said: an attractive woman. I could not look at her without wondering about the details of her intimate life with Lomas. It is a common belief that in the matter of sexual relations, it is the man who gets the most obvious and immediate relief : a relief therefore to which he commonly attaches more importance than the woman does – unless or until the woman is happily experienced or well taught. Had Isobel Fuller gone to Frank Lomas more for his sake than for her own? Was she experienced? How sensitively had Lomas managed to school her? Was it possible that, apart from the complications of his own abstinence, the lessons he had learned from Hetty Wilson had stood him in good stead? Presumably he had overcome the false guilt of associating the two women. There were questions about Isobel Fuller that I could not ask. And I could not solve them by simply looking at her. I dropped the stockings back on the pile.

'I suppose none of us is to be free from your obnoxious attention? And the more innocuous and uncomplaining we are, the longer will be our contribution to your time-sheet?'

I turned and saw that Fuller had come in behind us.

'Elimination,' I said. 'The sooner it's achieved, the more comfortably we can all talk.'

He grunted. There are two kinds of successful retired men. One attempts to carry over into private life the bustle and command to which he has become accustomed. The other will struggle, perhaps to the point of nervous disruption, to thrust these behind him. Fuller I placed in the second category, but making an aggressive excursion into the first in defence of his own.

'You too, if you don't mind,' I told him. 'What were you wearing yesterday?'

'What I'm wearing now.'

'You've changed your shirt, Father,' Isobel said. 'One or two other things too, I would hope.'

'I'll go and get them.'

'I'll come with you,' I said.

The things were crumpled in a heap still beside his bed. Isobel picked them up and handed them to me. I made my inspection look as desultory as possible – almost casual. But I took care to look at the places that might have been revealing: shirt front, shirt cuffs and socks above the ankle. There was no staining – no food, mud or blood.

'I must also ask you to tell me your movements last night.'

'I did not move from the drawing-room all evening.'

'Doubtless someone will testify to that?'

'Cook herself brought me a milky drink at half-past nine.'

'That sounds clear, then.'

Fuller looked at me, still smouldering. 'It's nothing of the sort, Inspector. If you are going to waste your time investigating my daughter and me, you might at least make a proper job of it. I had ample time between Isobel's going out and my night-cap to have gone to Dead-Nettle mine and hacked down a dozen camp-followers.'

'Good,' I said. 'That's even better. A plain lack of alibi can sometimes be more convincing than a nice schedule of witnesses.'

I looked in the direction of his daughter. We were pretty well through the distasteful preliminaries, and it could be important to me in the immediate future to be on easy terms with this pair. I expected now at least a glance of sympathetic assurance from her – but the look in her eyes had become strange. There was a general look of distraction that had not been there when I talked to her earlier. Fuller noticed it at once.

'Have you finished with my daughter now, Inspector?'

'For the time being.'

'I should go to your room, Isobel. I know you had a sleepless night. Don't just play at having a rest. Take your clothes off and get into bed. Inspector – if you and I might have a further word?'

'Of course.'

He took me down into the morning room where Lomas had first called on him and offered me claret and a biscuit, which I saw no reason to decline.

'Inspector – I can't see that you have any reason to be bullying Isobel.'

'I haven't been bullying her. One firm encounter, to clear up what had to be cleared up. Henceforward we can be purely constructive.'

'I would hope so. In theory, it must have occurred to you that Isobel might have felt inclined to kill this woman from Lomas's past.'

'That is why – '

'Only she didn't.'

He looked at me as if he were daring me to contradict him.

'I have to keep my mind open to all possibilities,' I said. 'But it's pretty well closed already to that one.'

'So I should hope. But there's something else that I want to say to you. If any evidence had come into my hands that would implicate Lomas, I would have been tempted to destroy it. I think I would rather pretend to be guilty myself, than see him face the music.'

Again the challenge: calculating eyes and a jutting chin. But he did not wait for me to rise to it.

'Because I am an ageing man, and I lost two years ago all that I had to lose. I do not know whether you have yet heard my story, and I do not propose to delay you with it now. When it does come to your ears, I hope you will linger between the lines long enough to understand something of what has been destroyed for me : enforced retirement, the death of my wife, this expensive paradise that has proved itself a white mammoth. Therefore I can lay some claim to knowing what Frank Lomas means to Isobel – in theory – and a good deal more about the actual facts than she would suppose. I cannot say that he was what I had initially wished for her. But that, I now think, was possibly my mistake. In fact, it is a mistake to have wishes at all in such matters.'

He sat back in his chair and achieved a greater degree of relaxation than I had seen in him before.

'Inspector, you are an intelligent man and I do not have to spell everything out for you. I am not saying that murder is an acceptable way out of any man's impasse. Let us simply say that it would be a pity if the killing of Mrs Lomas were followed by the wreckage of anyone else's life. That is why I fervently hope that you will fail in your present task – especially if the truth does in fact lie in a particular direction. Oh – you have no need to worry. Please do not think you have to lecture me on the gravity of obstructing you in the course of your duties. I would not really think of impeding you. I fear I am too timorous and ingrained in abiding by the law, ever to do otherwise.'

'You had met Mrs Lomas, had you?'

'No. But I had listened interminably to this man Slack, who tried months ago to drop sly innuendoes that there was some dry, hollow rattle in Lomas's cupboard. I vacillated between plain disbelief and the hope that whatever it was, it was over and done with. Slack is a worthless character, as Isobel has been trying to get me to admit since he arrived. My mind is now made up to get rid of him. I shall accept the timing from you in that matter.'

'In what sense?'

'I shall retain him long enough for you to know where he is if you need him.'

I found Slack and Burgess painting the doors and window-frames of a mid-Victorian stable that formed three sides of a square round a cobbled yard. Slack was what I expected him to be: a man trying to carry into mid-life something of the dapper and dashing impact that he had cultivated in his youth. There was so much physical activity still being forced on him that he was not yet running to fat; but he was beginning to spread. If ever he came into money, he would quickly degenerate. I put on him from the beginning the staccato professional pressure that I had spared all the others. I interrogated the pair of them with irritating repetitions and confusing pretences at misunderstanding. What were their movements yesterday evening?

'I'd wanted to talk to Frank Lomas, so Harry and I went to meet him from Chapel. At least, we knew where – '

'Stop. What did you want to talk to him about?'

'A business deal. I'd mentioned it to him before, but he hadn't wanted to play. But I knew things had been getting pretty desperate with him in his mine, and over here the old man had been getting on my wheel. It's time we all had a change. It had all been all right for the winter.'

Harry Burgess blinked vigorously in agreement.

'I was going to suggest a partnership. If I could only get Frank out of Dead-Nettle, there are plenty of mines round here worth working. Frank and I together – if Fuller would put up some working capital – '

'But Lomas wasn't at Chapel.'

'No. But as it happened, that didn't affect me. I had caught sight of Isobel, hanging about waiting for him, too, so it was obvious that this wasn't going to be the night for talking business. So I thought we'd go out and see Hetty Lomas. I'd known her before, you see, in the old days.'

He rolled his eyes in suggestive memory and Harry Burgess's flabby lower lip dropped in a grin.

'Known her in the old days? You'd been instrumental in bringing her up here, I believe.'

Slack shook his head. 'No, sir, No, sir, thank you very much. In the old days, down in Kent, we'd all mucked in together. But if you knew Hetty's husband – '

'Her husband? You're not talking about Lomas?'

Slack and Burgess exchanged secret amusement.

'No. Her real husband. Old Tug Wilson. Company Quartermaster-Sergeant with a battalion of the Buffs. Out on the Afghan frontier, while we were knocking about in Thanet, and God knows where he is now. But he comes round from time to time, and I wouldn't want to tangle with him.'

'You mean that the woman we've been calling Mrs Lomas was guilty of bigamy?'

'Haven't you forked that one out yet?'

'You'd better fork it out for me. And be quick about it.'

Slack laid aside his paint brush, which he had been holding as if I were not going to interrupt his work for long.

'She'd been married all the time. That's why she'd done her best to keep putting Frank off. She didn't mind casting around a favour or two: it was a long old lope from the Minster Marshes to the Khyber Pass. But she stopped short at that kind of complication.'

'In that case, Slack, you were partly responsible for compounding a felony.'

'No, sir, Mr Brunt. I compounded nothing – only a

joke. All we did was to pull old Frank's leg. You don't know what a bloody nit he was, in his early army days. Listen – I got him in and, honestly, I got so bloody sorry for him, I began to feel responsible. I helped him out of dozens of holes. It took them a month to teach him to march. He was one of those awkward sods who swung his right arm forward with his right leg, and the more the drill-sergeant got on to him, the more awkward he became. He was what was generally referred to as a part of the female anatomy – which is being less than fair to the girls.'

'Get back to Hetty Wilson, Slack.'

'Yes, well, she did her best to put Frank off, but he was one of those who believed in signing in a vestry for what he'd had. Then we suddenly heard – those of us who were in the know – that the battalion's sailing orders were through. We knew one of the Orderly Room clerks who wasn't beyond dropping us a fruity hint. And if you had any savvy, you could work things out for yourself. We knew from one of the officers' mess waiters just when the wine merchant's order was to be stopped. The farmer where we were camped was getting hot under his collar about the way we'd blocked off one of his hay-fields – but he'd had a quiet word we'd be out of his way in a fortnight.'

'Hetty Wilson, Slack.'

'Yes, well we said to her, "Put the poor bugger out of his misery," we said. "Maybe he'll have a Zulu warrior's spear up his jacksey before he's much older. Let them start giving the banns out. We'll be ground-baiting the Bay of Biscay by the third Sunday." '

'And it nearly worked?'

'Bloody nearly. If the padre hadn't stuck his nose in. I went round to see her the night before. We weren't supposed to break camp, but you had to be your own

154

master sometimes. She was packed up for off, but then the Senior Subaltern came to fix up a few things with her about tomorrow's details. She must have got bogged down with him. I don't know, because I had to make myself scarce. And I've got an idea she spent the night in officers' quarters. At any rate, she was on parade the next morning, dead scared, but too drunk to know what she was doing, anyway.'

Harry Burgess's mouth stayed open in second-to-second enjoyment of the tale.

'And you stayed in touch with her?'

'What, me? Find 'em, fool 'em and forget 'em. I don't mind admitting that I'd slipped in once or twice while Frank was out. She deserved a slow ride in-between times with that big old oaf, didn't she? But keep in touch? No. Too much respect for Tug Wilson.'

'Yet you brought her up to Margreave.'

'No.'

'How else could she have found Lomas's whereabouts?'

'I've wondered. The Regimental Depot, perhaps.'

'They'd have sent her straight here, not to a rendezvous in Derby.'

'I know. It's a bloody mystery to me,' Slack said.

'Not to me, it isn't. You brought her here to unearth a cache for you.'

Slack laughed. 'You've been listening to too much talk, Mr Brunt — and you only in the place an hour or two. There've always been strange tales about Dead-Nettle — and about me. You'd have a job to prove anything, Inspector.'

It was then that I determined, childish though it might be, that whatever the outcome of the main case, I was going to see Gilbert Slack home on some indictable count before I was finished.

'At least you won't deny that it was you who gave him the idea of mining Dead-Nettle in the first place.'

'We were pissed that night, both of us.'

'You told him –'

'How can I remember what I told him? We'd lived in each other's haversacks for three or four years. God knows what we did find to talk about.'

'Dead-Nettle.'

'He'd been a miner. He often used to tell us about it: hard-luck stories about roof-falls and the fire-damp. I told him there was easier money to be dug in Derbyshire. As there is – if you know where to look.'

'Which is not in Dead-Nettle.'

'I said the first name of a mine that I remembered. I'd no idea that he'd ever come up here. None of us could see much further than the next dawn.'

'He'd just saved your life, hadn't he, by shooting a farmer's wife?'

'He was trembling like a leaf when he'd done it. If he hadn't, you wouldn't have been talking to me today.'

That was the size of Gilbert Slack; not for a second had a thought of the Dutch woman ruffled him.

'So you think, speaking as man to man, that he had it in him to kill Hetty?'

'You've no right to ask me that.'

'You're his friend, or so you would have me believe. You can say what you think.'

I attached little importance to his verbal answer. But I watched his reaction; it could be informative. There was no way of being really sure, but what did he think, beneath all the bluff and the bluster? He had been a petty criminal all his life; he had talked his way out of dozens of scrapes. He was easy to read, but hard to catch.

I came to the conclusion that he believed Lomas was

the murderer; which would mean that he hadn't killed Hetty himself. But I went on with the appropriate motions.

'And no one told Lomas, in all your years together, that he had gone through an empty ceremony with a married woman?'

'Only Harry and I knew, and we held our tongues.'

I looked disbelieving, but Slack was firm on the point.

'Don't you see? Frank would have gone to the padre. We didn't want that sort of trouble.'

I jumped through time and space.

'So when you came away from the Chapel?'

'We thought it was the right time to go and see Hetty. We knew Frank was out and he didn't leave the mine often.'

'And you found – ?'

'I never saw anything that sickened me more in my life. Not even in the war.'

'So what did you do about it?'

'Cleared off out of it, mate. That's one thing we did learn in khaki: not to volunteer for anything, and never to get involved.'

At least, that rang true. But I was not sure about Gilbert Slack yet. Might not Hetty herself have found the loot? Might she not have decided to set something on one side for her own purposes?

Had Slack come upon her, yesterday evening, in the act of betraying him too?

CHAPTER NINETEEN

I went back to Derby at the end of that afternoon. What had happened there was an unknown quantity. I did not understand why Hetty Wilson had gone there in the first place. I could not see why, if she had wanted to re-attach herself to Frank, she had not simply come up to him in Margreave. And Frank had been vague about it. He only knew what Hetty had told him, and she had not told him much. She had been afraid of him, she claimed; afraid of what her reception might be; she could not face him until they had exchanged letters. It was feasible; I would put it no higher. It did not convince me.

And how had she found her way to Emma Rice's? For a woman needing to go to ground in a strange town, with tailor-made shadows to hide in available at a price, the scrofulous boarding-house was ideal. Emma Rice did not ask questions; she did not have to. She made sure she already knew all the answers. She dropped enough crumbs our way, in the normal course of events, to keep herself out of trouble without besmirching her own reputation. So how had Hetty Wilson even heard of her?

I waylaid P.C. Kewley and brow-beat him until we had reconstructed the meeting between Lomas and the woman in the middle of the road, the ambush that had never happened, with Duncan Mottershead and his minions pinned down under their cover. Our office was frustratingly deserted that evening. I wanted to set colleagues on the track of the stranger who was said to have stayed at the *Bell Inn. Ex military*, Kewley had said, *or a flat-catcher trying to look like one*. Not much doubt now who that had been.

I bought a port and lemon for Tilly Sutcliffe and obtained from her confirmation of much that I already knew. It was not very helpful. Much of Tilly's so-called information was as speculative as mine, and not very bright speculation at that. I felt fairly certain that the manner in which Hetty Wilson had almost fallen into the hands of Mottershead and his footpads was coincidental to our main concern. Mottershead might have known nothing about Hetty Wilson, might merely have looked on her as potential competition – of some strength! – for his own string of girls. So she would be offered the choice of joining his own team or being seen out of town. One of the odd things about Hetty, in Mottershead's eyes, must have been her lack of a protector. He must have had his worries about the letter that she was obviously waiting for. The advent of a new, and to judge from Hetty's quality, somewhat choosey ponce at the back of St Mary's Gate could have been very disturbing to Mottershead. Or his target might have been much more simple. Robbery with violence was something that happened as and where opportunity offered. Perhaps he thought she might have been carrying the proceeds from pawning another bracelet.

A cluster of irrelevancies: or were they? I needed to know. It was a strange thing, the effect on a strange town of a woman like Hetty Wilson. I had met others like her in my life: one or two. Wherever they moved, worlds seemed to fall apart all around them, without any effort on their part. A man who takes up with one of them has virtually shot his albatross. Probably Mottershead and his women had been acting purely on something they had sensed.

I went to see Emma Rice, in itself a tricky business. I would rather have been taken there by one of my colleagues in the town. We have an agreement about her. She is useful to some, so others are not encouraged to look too closely. Besides, too many of us might confuse her. The Derby inspector would have hated it if ever her boarding-house had been closed down. It formed a very useful focal point.

Emma Rice and I knew each other, of course; and she did not like me. She did not trust me. But just for once she behaved as if she had been expecting me: as perhaps she had. The murder of Hetty Wilson had reached the evening papers.

She was pathetically grieved by it. I sat through the rebarbative spectacle of a fat and monumentally immovable woman, sniffing at a sodden twist of handkerchief that she had brought up from somewhere in her accumulation of pleats and folds.

'And such a pretty child.'

It was always a matter of passing interest what act Emma would put on during any particular visit. Even her legitimate business deals were carried on under some pretence or other.

'You must have talked to her a lot,' I said. 'I gather that she didn't go out much.'

'She was afraid to. A country girl – in all the town traffic. Even from here to the Post Office and back was a torment to her.'

'Oh, yes? And I also gather that someone was dogging her steps?'

She puckered her brow. Emma Rice's skin was very white. Her multiple chins hardly moved when she talked.

'She didn't say anything to me about that. Too modest,

perhaps. A girl like that would find men's steps quickening behind her wherever she went, wouldn't she? Believe me, it used to happen to me once.'

'I was thinking of something more personal. Someone she was afraid of. Someone she knew, and had been more than half expecting.'

'If there was anything like that, Mr Brunt, it didn't come to my ears.'

'It's being said that someone tried to call for her here – a man.'

'Who's saying that?'

It was time I showed a little authority. By way of answer, I simply stared her out. She did not have to let that affect her – but now she put on all the facial accompaniment of remembering something.

'A man did come to the door while she was here – but it was not her he was looking for. He had caught sight of her and mistaken her for someone else.'

'You allowed him to confront her, did you?'

'Mr Brunt, a hotel has to protect the privacy of its guests. I spoke to him myself.'

'What sort of man?'

If she had said that he had two arms, two legs, two eyes and one nose, she could not have told me less. She was constructively unhelpful, and yet contrived to put her last reserves of gravity into the description.

'And why was she staying in Derby, Mrs Rice? What was she waiting for?'

'I'm sure you must already know all about that, Inspector.'

'I would like to compare the story she told you with what she told other people.'

She sighed, as if this talking was a physical imposition. 'That she had left her husband in a girlish rage and had written asking his forgiveness. She was waiting his reply.'

I waited.

'Poor young thing,' she added. 'I told her any man would be a fool not to want her back. But then she was worried in case he might think it was only his money she was after.'

'His money?'

'He has made good with a mine, it seems, in the hills out Wirksworth way. I told her not to be so silly. Money's no good to a man, if he hasn't a wife to help him spend it.'

I still waited.

'That's all there is to tell, Mr Brunt.'

'It isn't. I want to know how she came to stay here in the first instance. Who made the arrangements? How did she ever come to hear of you?'

This time she paused before replying. 'It's funny you should ask me that, Mr Brunt.'

'Not funny at all, Mrs Rice.'

'I was out at the market when someone came. The entry was in the book when I came back. One of the cleaners had written it in. Although they are strictly forbidden – '

She thrust one of her hands under herself. Her flesh overflowed from her chair – from which, in fact, she seldom ever moved. I did not believe that she ever went to market. She conducted her manifold businesses from where she sat, and most of her working paraphernalia seemed to be tucked away about her, in folds of fat or clothing. She seemed actually to be sitting on the register of visitors. She brought it out and showed me the entry of Hetty Wilson's booking. It was written in a different hand from the others: large, printed letters, barely literate.

'Please tell me the name of this cleaner, and her address.'

'It'll do you no good, Mr Brunt. She's what you'd call simple.'

I insisted, for form's sake, on noting the details. Then I gave up. I heard the click of billiard balls in an adjacent room. I wondered if she had a public licence for the game. If not, I could pull her in under Section 11 of the Gaming Act of 1845. That was the extent of the depth to which my mind was sinking. I put the thought from me and went to scribble a few operational notes to colleagues in the office.

I was about to go home when P.C. Kewley came in – in mufti. I knew I had roasted him on to his mettle, and had expected him to get down to some work in his private time. But I had not expected results as quickly as this.

'Found who he is, sir. The books at the *Bell* are straightforward enough. A man called Wilson.'

No surprise. It fell flat on my ears.

'We'll have to have him traced, Constable Kewley.'

'Shouldn't be difficult, sir. I have his home address too, from the register, and everything has an above-board look about it. Aldershot, Hants.'

Hetty's legitimate husband seemed on the face of it to be leading an open and legitimate existence. I was becoming unused to the idea that anyone ever did.

CHAPTER TWENTY

Sergeant Clayton, whom I had left in charge at Margreave during my short absence, was not one of my
familiars. A newcomer to my section from the Stafford-
shire borders, I had no working knowledge of him –
beyond the certainty that if Rouse at Swadlincote had
put him up for promotion, he must have shown himself
willing to pull weight. He was a quiet type, did not
argue, did not even ask questions. I hoped that this was
because he had no need to. I left him with only the
broadest of guide-lines; no specific targets and no pro-
hibitions. I let him know that I did regard it as important
to keep an ostentatious eye on the movements, if
possible also the intentions, of those whom we could not
arrest, but did not want to pass from our ken. I also
privately hoped that he would not upset by tactless
interview those with whom I prided myself on having
made initial progress. I did not care for the thought of
having to make a difficult second start with Frank Lomas
or Isobel Fuller. But I did not say this aloud. While I
was away, he must do what he saw needed to be done.
Clayton could make his first mistake before I started
hounding him.

He met me with the news that Isobel Fuller had been
taken ill. At first I took it that this was due to the full
shock as comprehension took hold through her fatigue.
And I suppose that this was what it was – though no
mere pallid collapse. Clayton let it patiently sink in
on me that she really was disorientated. Her father –
with whom he had worked up a case-work friendship –
had told him that she was not even talking continuous
sense. He had called in their doctor, who had insisted

on isolating her *incommunicado*. And if this did not actually settle any problems for us, it did at least relieve us of some indecision. I would have dearly liked some knowledge of the content of her delirium, but it was not easy to come by. I told Clayton to question her father and to pump the servants as and when he could, without making a meal of it. I knew how little we could rely on a mixture of rumour and misinterpretation, several times removed from source. Isobel Fuller was effectively inaccessible to us for the time being; but at least immobilised.

Two people had been fretting for me during my absence and were pleading for interviews immediately on my return. One was Frank Lomas, and I was gratified to be occupying already the position of chief mentor-in-waiting to him. But I was not sure where to put him on my scale of priorities. Lomas was obviously going to take up a good deal of my time, once I made a proper start on him.

'Does he seem in confessional mood?' I asked Clayton.

'Bursting to unburden,' Clayton said. 'Of everything short of murder.'

That was as I thought.

'And do you think he is our murderer, Sergeant?'

Clayton was still in the stage of treating my questions with hyper-prudence. But he understood that I really did want an answer.

'It seems silly, sir – but it seems to me that if he were, he wouldn't be able to keep it to himself.'

'Not silly at all, Sergeant.'

The other supplicant was Florence Belfield, and I chose to see her first because as far as I was concerned, she did at least represent something new. I feared from what I had heard of her that I was in for nothing more than a chaos of hallucinations, but what attracted me to her, in my innocence, was that she was the one person in Margreave who was a law unto herself. Making any sense of what she said might be akin to Lomas's efforts to chip metal out of the gangue; but there might be crude ore there.

I was in for a morning of surprises, and Florence Belfield provided some of them. Her cottage was situated, as Lomas's was, within the working radius of an old mine, a single shaft covered with a none too robust wooden hatch, on which stood primitive winding-gear : her stowe. Decades ago, this had been nicked : tally-marks had been cut by the Bar Master at three three-weekly intervals, as a warning that he was dispossessing her. But as there had been no other takers for Badger's Swallet, she had been allowed to remain indefinitely in the dwelling-house.

I could only make a guess at her age. She must have been well into her seventies, which meant she had been living in Badger's since before the Crimean War, when the interior of Africa was still an empty query on the map, and our present King a boy in his teens. She looked brittle, and moved about as an old woman moves; but one had the impression that there were reserves here that she was consciously and jealously guarding for the day when she might need them. In her twenties. following the mining death of her husband, she had inspired and directed an underground war with all its ramifications. In her thirties she had been narrowly saved from drowning in a flooded gallery. Thereafter she had lived on a plane of terror-dreams in a state of alarming penury. Her very survival seemed to have been largely the product of her will.

Nevertheless, the interior of her cottage bore witness to a certain sense of order. It looked like the home of a woman in whose life a lot was going on. It was not clean, it was not tidy, but it was tolerable. She knew where to find things. There were plans, rolled and unrolled, of her own and neighbouring workings. There were rock specimens on a table, a pestle and mortar with partially crushed ore. There was a blue-print for a now out-of-date beam-engine that might have been used for draining a hillside. If only her husband had lived, the hills about Margreave might have been in a different condition today.

In her talk the past ran indistinguishably into the present. She knew that a woman had been recently killed in Dead-Nettle, though she did not, of course, know who she was. And it did not seem to trouble her at all, this mixture of knowing and not-knowing. She knew that Frank Lomas was struggling – and failing – to work the mine. She did not remember his name, yet she spoke openly and clearly of the visit she had paid him and she was angry with him because he had not yet, as he had promised, been down to call on her. Yet she could not have said the first thing about him, and accepted her own ignorance as if it was all part of the will of fate – like the alarums and excursions of mine warfare in which she believed herself to be still caught up.

She knew, too, that I was a policeman, with a footing in stronger places than Margreave. And as I had feared, she wanted to lay information about the villainy of local unworthies, now most of them dead. She was not easily put off: in fact she would not be put off at all, and in the last lap, when she discovered that I was just another of officialdom's born non-co-operators, I knew I would have to face the wrath of the true virago.

But for the moment my main concern was not to offend her. Her strange *mélange* of reason and unreason had a peculiar effect on her fantasies. She had a remarkable command of detail when she was dealing with what was real, and she applied this with equal vigour to her fantasies. Consequently an unwarned stranger on first encounter might be tempted into action by every word she said.

'This man at Dead-Nettle had another man to help him a week or two ago.'

'What other man?'

'The man with the moustache. But they did not stay long in partnership. Barely a morning. I could hear them shouting at each other. The sound travels strangely in some of these underground places.'

'Where were you, then, when you heard them?'

'In Badger's.'

She seemed surprised that I should have to ask.

'You still go down into the mine, sometimes, do you?'

A bad mistake. I could feel her vexation. She was about to dismiss me as being as useless as the rest.

'I'm still working it.'

Was she incapable of differentiating between her two worlds?

'Mrs Belfield, I think you might be able to help me.'

'It seems to me that the boot ought to be on the other foot.'

'It was you who were the first to discover the dreadful thing that had happened in Dead-Nettle.'

'He'd hit her with one of his gads, Mr Brunt – beaten her with it again and again, as if he were whipping her with a thong.'

'You didn't actually see him hitting her, did you?'

She went on talking as if she had not heard the questions. Was this to avoid giving me an answer that might disappoint me?

'It was that Wilbur Thorpe. He used to work for me, but then he went over to Dead-Nettle. That was when Simon Hartle still had the freedom. Before this new man. Long before this new man. I distinctly heard Wilbur Thorpe's voice.'

A long time before the new man. She raised my hopes for a moment, but it seemed likely that Wilbur Thorpe was another of those long departed. As a matter of form, I looked him up later in the church register. He was buried in 1863.

'That was one of the things I was going to ask you,' I said. 'What made you go over to Dead-Nettle on a night like that?'

'I told you, didn't I? I heard voices.'

'How many voices did you hear?'

'Well, let me see, who does Simon Hartle have working for him? There's Wilbur Thorpe and Albert Boardman, Billy Orgill and young Tommy Dawson.'

'You heard them all, did you?'

Again she did not answer. Were there moments when she caught sight herself of the fact that she was talking nonsense?

'That's all you heard, was it, voices? You heard them from in here, did you? From inside this cottage?'

'It was a terribly dark night, Mr Brunt. I had to go across the yard. And I could see lights shining across the hollow, in all the windows, up at Dead-Nettle. And the door was standing open. I could see the light shining round that, too. Then I heard the woman scream. She'd screamed before, a night or two ago. He must have been beating her. He must have beaten her the other night, too. But not with a gad that time.'

For a moment I thought I might still win. She was reliving Sunday night.

'I climbed the hill as fast as I could towards Dead-Nettle deads. But I got there too late. I heard him ride away on his horse while I was still only half way there.

When I arrived, the door was still open and she was lying there like something on a butcher's slab.'

I took her through it again, but added nothing new to my knowledge. She started to bring Wilbur Thorpe into the story again, so I tried to move to fresh ground.

'Mrs Belfield, you spoke just now about the man who came to work for a morning with Frank Lomas at Dead-Nettle. They were never in partnership. This other man did not stay much longer than an hour. But you have no idea at all who he was?'

'He was a stranger in Margreave.'

'He wasn't, Mrs Belfield. He was a young man whom I think you know very well.'

'Tell me his name, then.'

'Gilbert Slack.'

She looked at me, puzzled.

'Tiggy Slack's son, Mrs Belfield.'

'Gilbert. Gilbert Slack,' she said. 'Gilbert Slack's been long gone from here. Gone for a soldier.'

'And come back, Mrs Belfield. I'm surprised you didn't recognise him.'

'I never saw him up close. I only heard his voice.'

'Yet you told me he had a moustache.'

She saw the reason behind this, but it was when reason stepped in that she seemed most puzzled.

'Gilbert Slack is a bad man, Mr Brunt. He was a bad boy.'

She got up and opened a cupboard from which she brought out an old sack, which she emptied on to the table: electro-plated trays and sugar bowls. There were a few articles in solid silver: toilet and trinket boxes, an ornate ink-stand, a napkin-ring and a cigar-case in rolled gold.

'Gilbert Slack is a robber, Mr Brunt. It was Gilbert Slack who had hidden all these.'

If young Slack had thought that he was hoarding a fortune here, then he must have been as impressionable as Frank Lomas at his most naïve. It was all lower middle-class finery : not worth more than a few pounds at the most.

'Where did you find all this, Mrs Belfield ?'

'In Dead-Nettle. I had to go there, you see, because Wilbur Thorpe was up to no good in there.'

'When was this, Mrs Belfield ?'

'After Gilbert Slack went away. After he went into the army. But I didn't take them for myself, Mr Brunt. I brought them away for safe-keeping. They've been in my cupboard ever since.'

'Where exactly did you find them ?'

'In a coffer, under the gravel, at the far end of the stope, where the Old Man gave up.'

'You did well, Mrs Belfield.'

I got away from her at last and went over to Dead-Nettle with the sack over my shoulder like some barn-storming ham actor. Uppermost in my mind was that I could hardly put Florence Belfield in as evidence, that I would need something firmer than that to tie up a case against Gilbert Slack. I was thinking about him too much still. Had I not been paying so much attention to the poetic satisfaction of putting him away, it might have sunk in on me earlier that Florence Belfield had actually put me in possession of a vital thought that could lead me to the killer of Hetty Wilson. It was the second time, in fact, that this clue had been laid before me. But for the moment I did not see it. Negative evidence does sometimes blinker one.

I went to see Frank Lomas and found him in the act of creating an even more austere tidiness about his home. He was in fact actually packing up his furniture and boxes, leaving out only the barest essentials of everyday life. I noticed that the things that had come over from the Fullers – the Grecian vase, the gilt picture-frames from which his family photographs had now been removed – had been neatly set apart on top of one of his chests. His mining tools were tied in a bundle.

'Not thinking of leaving us, I hope?'

'Not till you give me the word, Mr Brunt. But I'll not stay an hour longer, once you've given me the right-away.'

'And you've made up your mind what you're going to do with yourself?'

'Not yet, I haven't. That's something I'm putting off till the very last moment. I'm afraid, though, I know only too well what it's going to be.'

He tried to smile.

'That's hardly like you, Frank – not facing up to things as they are.'

'I've done a lot of things in my time that are not like me, Mr Brunt.'

'I suppose we all have, from time to time.'

And then he started. I was with him four or five hours. I heard much that I already knew, and much that I didn't: about coal-mines and infantry camps, about fear and high spirits in military action, even about the poetry – *it was the only way to look at it, Mr Brunt* – of improvised sanitation. About Hetty Wilson and Isobel Fuller. He told me things about both the women that sharpened my understanding of them – and of himself. He wasn't a man, I thought, who would ever know what to make of women. His only hope was to find one he could trust. He used me as a sounding-board for his own simple ethics. Most of all, he wanted to look on himself as guiltless. I tried in vain to make him see that *guilt*, as he saw it, was of no great importance. He did not

172

tell me anything that helped me to name the killer of Hetty Wilson.

'But if I were you, Frank, I'd delay my departure until certain things – '

'I've already told you, Mr Brunt: I'm not running away. You've no need to worry.'

'I'm not worried, Frank. I'm certain you committed no crime here.'

'Then there's no point in my staying. There's no lead in Dead-Nettle.'

'I'm not talking about lead. Dead-Nettle's shown you the way to something more abiding than a cartload of lead.'

'If you're talking about that stuff that Gilbert is supposed to have hidden away, Mr Brunt, you must know that I wouldn't have touched it.'

'That I do know – if for no other reason than that I have it all in this sack. You couldn't keep a wife for a fortnight on what it's worth.'

'My wife's dead, Mr Brunt.'

'And I wasn't thinking of her, either.'

He saw then at last what I meant, but shook his head in determined gloom.

'That's all over, Mr Brunt. You're talking about Isobel? It has to be all over. I couldn't ask her – '

He couldn't even put it in words to me.

'I think that the decision ought to be at least partially hers, Frank – *ultimately*. You'll notice I said *ultimately*.'

'What, me? A married man?'

'You weren't even that,' I said. 'You never were a married man. She wasn't entitled to go through a form of marriage with you.'

'All the same – '

It did not sink in on him at once. He had rejected Hetty Wilson when he realised she was no more than a camp follower. When he met her in that Derby street, he saw her for nearly all she was. But even then he hadn't known that she was a married woman. Even now I was not sure that he had grasped it. Eventually it might help, given his kind of conscience.

'All the same,' I said, in a completely different tone from his. And he thought about it, earnestly. I cannot really say that any positive hope appeared in his face – but I think his hopelessness was marginally relieved.

I left him working it all out afresh. If I knew anything about Frank Lomas's innate optimism, he would not give up without trying again.

CHAPTER TWENTY-ONE

Leitmotif – My sergeant and I were discussing the case in almost desultory fashion in a quiet corner of the *Adventurers' Arms* when ex-Company Quartermaster-Sergeant Wilson came in, and in the manner of most late afternoon arrivals in Margreave asked for a bed for the night.

He came in and stood for three seconds just within the door, taking stock of the geography of furniture and clientele. It was almost as if he were given to systematic reconnaissance of all the commonplaces in his life. It had been the same, we learned, when he had arrived at Wirksworth railway station : he had stood in the doorway of the Booking Hall looking out across the grey street as if he had never seen a provincial

English town before. In point of fact, we discovered, he had been in the army so long, if one includes civilian clerical duties at his Regimental Depot, that he had developed what almost amounted to a fear of any walk of life that diverged from his familiar patterns.

They knew at once in the *Adventurers' Arms* who he was. There was something almost of a caricature of the discharged soldier in his appearance; the ramrod bearing, the scathing eye for the cut of a civilian's moleskin trousers, the suppressed anger at the sloppiness of a world in which he hardly trusted himself to express an opinion. As P.C. Kewley had said of him, when he had been wandering the streets of Derby, usually at least half an hour's march behind Hetty's shadow, he looked, if not a retired soldier, at least like a confidence trickster posing as one.

We had dug out various accounts of the way he had comported himself in Derby in the days before Lomas had come to collect his wife. The memories of people in the town had become relaxed and lubricated once the daily newspapers had started crying for the arrest of Frank Lomas.

Wilson had stayed at the *Bell Inn*, had exchanged words with hardly anyone, but had looked penetratingly into the face of everyone he met: dark little eyes, stagnant with the suspicion engendered by his lack of intelligence, ready to believe that every man he met was in league with his cuckolders.

He spent most of his time in a slow patrol of the streets, always on the outer edge of the pavement, halting at intervals to face outwards for minutes at a time, scanning the faces of people about their daily round, peering in at the windows of cabs. Yet he questioned no one: he seemed convinced that sooner or later he must find her for himself.

And find her he did. It happened that he was watching the daily comings and goings of the town from the neighbourhood of the Post Office when he saw her come out from one of her vain visits to the *Poste Restante*. A mid-morning parcel-postman came between them with his red wicker handcart. He dodged bad-temperedly round it, but she had gained ten yards on him and a brewer's dray, lumbering behind her, cut him off from her as she crossed the road. He was away after her as fast as he could : and then for the next few vital minutes was in the wake of the wrong woman.

But at least the direction of Hetty's flight had turned his thoughts in the direction of St Mary's Gate. He caught sight of her again the next day, and she spotted him in time to turn smartly to the right along a flagged passage between tenements. He was harder on her heels this time. She turned left into a complex of warehouse yards, began to run, her heels and ankles kicking outwards unathletically under her hitched-up skirts. He began to double, and would undoubtedly have caught her had he not slipped badly on the iron heel of what look suspiciously like a pair of boots from army stores. And meanwhile his progress was being watched with delight by pairs of eyes of which he was unaware: men at work amongst crates and boxes, a labourer re-aligning cobbles disrupted by the winter's frosts. Wilson slithered round another right-angled corner to find the long, narrow alley deserted where a second previously he had seen her head bobbing over irregular spaces in the wall. He tried one after another of the nearest doors and gates, saw only waste spaces, discarded bits of machinery, a patchwork of arid allotments and a length of canal wharf.

Wilson lost her for the remainder of that day, but kept watch as doggedly as did Duncan Mottershead.

The next morning he saw her, or thought he saw her, coming out of Emma Rice's. He called on Emma, was received by her on her monumental throne, the fat of her bosom heaving like a mouse-ridden harmonium. No, she had no guest at the moment answering to the description of Hetty. She did not convince him, and he tried to stand his ground. But all these young ladies, these days, Emma wheezed, they looked so alike, especially when glimpsed from behind, on the further pavement. The white skin of her brow furrowed as she tried to think which of her visitors he might have mistaken for her.

Wilson by now was certain. Emma Rice's involvement was transparent – and yet impenetrable. He knew of no tactics other than a frontal attack; but Emma Rice was frustratingly just not amenable to verbal assault. He was about to lose his temper – which could not have advanced his cause in any way – when someone came in at the front door : a girl in the better-found servant class, in the long skirts and floppy hat of the age.

'Is that you, Jane ?'

Emma Rice called her up to her chair, not openly for Wilson's inspection, but clearly with no other underlying intention. And it was true : at a distance, and from behind, he might have mistaken her for Hetty.

'You got the currant loaf ?'

The girl answered and swung away. Emma Rice was a ruthless opportunist.

'She's the one you saw come out of the front door. About ten minutes ago, you said ?'

He thought he saw Hetty several times, later that morning, but every time a head was turned, he had the shock of discovering another unfamiliar face.

Before Wilson showed up in Margreave, I had sent

out requests to some of our colleagues in southern England to try to help us to piece together something of his background and of the circumstances of his marriage to Hetty. He had met her, a fetching and apparently ingenuous young thing, about a year before she stepped into the life of Frank Lomas, at a Sergeants' Mess Dance whilst his battalion was mustering for departure to India. Of Hetty herself little positive information came to light, beyond that she was a village girl, indeed from Hampshire, estranged from her parents for reasons which one can only – but all too easily – guess. And she was known to have arrived by train with other girls at other places where Her Majesty's troops were formally gathered.

The marriage with Wilson appears to have been completely out of character for both of them. Wilson was the last N.C.O. in his mess of whom romance was expected – a colourless, conservative, almost staid martinet of an infantry store-keeper. It is obvious that Hetty was an explosion in his life, but what she herself thought she had to gain from the match it is impossible to grasp. Some Quartermaster Sergeants, it is true, are excellent providers for others besides the troops in their care. She may even have wanted to impress, in some peculiar way and for some peculiar purpose, some of the women with whom she was doing the garrison rounds. Perhaps she was even looking ahead to a time when she might settle down. The last theory I can easily believe is that she was at any time genuinely in love with him; but even that, I suppose, is possible.

At any rate, by the time Wilson's discharge was imminent – that is to say, some years after Frank Lomas had been found, fooled, and already forgotten – she had cleared the decks of her interim commitments and entanglements. Wilson himself was taken on as a records-clerk in his own Regimental Depot, and they lived for a while in a rented cottage just beyond the perimeter of barrack life : the only life, it is clear, in which Wilson felt at ease. Our spies did not penetrate marital walls, and I have no way of knowing the inner secrets of the couple. They are not too difficult to imagine. Wilson was entirely inflexible – and so, in a totally different way, was Hetty. I think that she must also have pressed domestic ambitions on him. He had a day in London to face an Interview Board of the Corps of Commissionaires; perhaps he had already seen the desirability of taking Hetty away from even the sight of a barracks. When he returned home that evening, it was to find the cottage cold and deserted.

Wilson stood now at the bar of the *Adventurers' Arms*, his eyes scanning each of the drinkers in turn. And they were struck silent. They had had some recent practice in the reception of remote strangers but this one, they knew with one accord, was likely to prove a key figure. And the dramatic fact was not lost on them that Sergeant Clayton and I were surveying it all from our shadowy corner.

'Is there a man here who goes by the name of Gil?'

Nobody answered him, but two or three pairs of eyes looked over towards my sergeant and me, expecting some signal reaction. Wilson mistook their meaning and came over to us with stumpy, aggressive steps. He addressed himself to me.

'You are this Gil, are you?'

And he looked scornfully at Sergeant Clayton.

'And you, I supose, are Harry Burgess?'

I pulled out a chair for him and opened my wallet to show him my identity.

'I'm sorry, Inspector.'

He sank wearily beside us. Ex-CQMS Tug Wilson had drawn abreast with events at last: almost. All he knew, he had gathered from the newspapers. He assumed that Frank Lomas was the guilty man.

'And to tell you the truth, Inspector, I don't know whether to bash his own head in for him, or to shake him by the hand.'

'I'd do my best to forget about him altogether, if I were you,' I said. He told us about the cold, deserted cottage – and about the charred letter, in the empty grate, of which he had been able to salvage little more than two words: *Derby* and *Gil*. That was what had got Wilson as far as an audience with Emma Rice.

Could Wilson, masquerading his slow thought and belated arrivals, have been leading a second existence? I tried to project him into the role of murderer. I have always found this a valuable theoretical exercise – at any rate, often a sobering one – when an investigation has been stuck at a certain stage.

Could Wilson's private enquiries possibly have led him, earlier and in secret, to Margreave and Dead-Nettle? Could he have been here on Sunday night? Have been here and gone again? If he had ridden into the village, under cover of darkness, he could easily have steered clear of witnesses. And now he came here with this aspect of bumbling dignity, verging on the slow-witted. Couldn't it all be the perfect cover for him?

If he had ridden –

Good God – wasn't that the key to the whole story? Twice in her statements – once in this pub, when she had come here hysterical from her find in Dead-Nettle, and later to me, when I talked to her in Badger's Swallet, Florence Belfield had been certain that the intruder had ridden away from the mine on horse-back.

So it couldn't have been Frank Lomas, could it, because he hadn't a horse, and twice to my knowledge had had to hire one. It couldn't be Slack, because he had been on foot that evening, his main purpose having been to meet Lomas from Chapel and take him off somewhere. Likewise Isobel Fuller.

On my left-hand side, Sergeant Clayton was too well trained to stir a limb or meet my eyes. But I knew what he would be thinking. I now had enough information to make medicine with Gilbert Slack. It was Sergeant Clayton who had unearthed the bib-and-brace salesman, the one who had overheard the talk between Gilbert and Hetty. It was not lost on Clayton that I had been a good deal more anxious than any cool and objective Detective-Inspector ought to be to lay some positive charge against Slack – even if it were such a humdrum standby as obstructing us in the performance of our duties. With Wilson's evidence about the burnt letter in the grate, I was now in a position to mix Slack a fair old bottle. If I had anything to gain from it.

And one thought led fortuitously to another, wiping away an obstacle that had been troubling me all along. Why had Slack made Hetty wait in Derby? Why had he not let her come and take Lomas by storm here in Margreave?

Surely because Slack, thick-skinned and insensitive, unable to believe that his own charms could be resisted for long, must have had his eye on the day when, with Frank out of the way, he could turn his attentions to Isobel. And if Lomas had actually been away to fetch Hetty, how much more acrimoniously Isobel would have hated him.

That, I thought, fitted in very neatly with Slack's understanding of people.

The door of the inn opened again and Fordyce came in, my Detective-Constable, who had spent all his time on the case keeping a quiet eye on the movements of Frank Lomas.

'I think you ought to know, sir – Lomas has gone over to the Hall.'

That was the moment I had really been waiting for.

CHAPTER TWENTY-TWO

He rode away on horse-back –

The thought was gnawing continuously into my mind. I could be wrong about it, hopelessly and foolishly wrong. I am not claiming that it was the vital piece of evidence on which the case broke. But it was the vital point on which my thoughts turned. Yet I knew that I could be carpeted with ridicule for paying more than a fleeting heed to anything from Florence Belfield's lips.

But there were other things as well, other lines of thought to which my mind kept turning. Had I not myself been present at that strange moment that seemed, in retrospect, like the beginnings of Isobel's illness, while I had been examining the laundry for give-away stains?

There seemed a new advancement in the spring as I walked across the park to Margreave Hall: a warmer shaft of sunshine than had so far blessed the Low Peak in this month of March. But it did not suffuse me with lyrical hope. Summer and fruition would come to these fields in season. But yet another life – I was not thinking now of Hetty Wilson – was as good as over.

Someone had ridden away on horse-back? Why was I being so stupidly confident that Slack, and Lomas, and Isobel, had come to the cottage on foot? Might not Lomas, leaving the chapel – or either of the other two, abandoning their intention to meet him as he came out – have gone on foot to Fuller's stables to get a horse?

Why should they? Because they knew in advance that they would be wanting to make a quick get-away? Something of my sense of relief departed from me.

As I came within sight of the Hall, I saw that Slack and Burgess had at last begun work on that fallen statuary. Cupids and shepherds, discus-throwers and poised Olympian athletes with javelins missing from their outstretched arms had been raised on their pedestals, but not yet transferred to their final posts. They had been right-dressed in a ludicrous military line.

Within the Hall a new regime was making itself felt, even to the eyes of a relatively detached observer. Desperately incapable of nursing his daughter himself, Esmond Fuller had sent for his deceased wife's sister, a mindless meddler, a mistress of the art of making herself indispensable. I do not mean to imply that she was making a set at Fuller himself. She was one of those women who cannot conceive that anyone should not comply with her will; and yet about her will, mostly an accumulation of trivialities, there was no discernible philosophy. As she took off her coat in any house, her pattern established itself about her. She took me into her morning room and Esmond Fuller was sitting with his mid-morning claret and biscuit, his wine-table set on the wrong side of his chair. There was no immediate sign of Frank Lomas about the house. I presumed – and hoped – that he had been allowed up to the sick-room.

'How's the patient?'

'On the better side, I think,' Fuller said. 'But beyond my reach.'

When I looked at him for enlightenment, he got up and walked about the room, without, I think, really knowing that he had left his chair.

'I may as well tell you. Our doctor has no nonsense about keeping confidences from those who might be able to help – even if he does pay lip-service to wrapping them up. She will improve rapidly as she settles down to her condition, that's how he put it.'

He looked at me as if uncertain whether I would grasp this.

'So now you know. And so do I. And I am not surprised, I am not disgusted. My sister-in-law is disgusted. I am doing my best to feel glad.'

'Lomas is with her now?'

He nodded, a trifle vacantly. 'On Monday, just after you left, I thought I had lost her altogether. Tuesday the same. She could not talk continuous sense. She seemed to have returned to childhood. I listened in vain for anything that she might let slip. But there was nothing. And I was surprised at her collapse. She was the last person on earth I would have expected to go under.'

'She has had a lot to carry.'

And he took this very gravely.

'Too much. And it was beyond me to cope. I sent for Dorothy.'

He did not complain about, hardly even seemed to notice, the vexations that had been brought into his way of life.

'On Wednesday she was suddenly much better. A woman of remarkable resilience, as I had always thought. Remarkably better – only she would not admit it to me. She just lay there, looking at us – her aunt, the doctor, me. You could see that her eyes were clear again. She knew where she was, and I think she had pieced together most of what must have happened. Her eyes were watching us, but she did not seem able to bring herself to talk.'

'She's talked since?'

'Not a word.'

'Let's hope Lomas puts that right,' I said. 'I have been waiting for him to make the move. I have known all along that he had it in him. Like the time, I am sure you have heard the story, when he stood on the authority of his two stripes.'

'Because he knew he was entitled to them. Or suddenly felt he was, for the first time.'

'You've come to a very clear understanding of him,' I said.

'An honest man. And what else would a man look for, for his daughter? And apart from that sort of sentimentality, they have everything ahead of them. I shall not always be here, and I do not know what they will make of this place. But they cannot go wrong. If only – '

'If only I would go away,' I said. 'That will not be until my work is finished, Mr Fuller.'

'You can do no good here, Mr Brunt. You may satisfy the law, but the law won't remember with any sense of gratitude. I doubt whether you'll even succeed in bringing a conviction. There's too much blood and mud on everybody's boots.'

'But not on everybody's reins and saddles,' I said.

'I wouldn't know about that.'

'How honest is an honest man?' I asked him.

'I was never brought up to believe that there were varying degrees of truth.'

'Honest enough to come forward of his own accord,

if I were to make a wrong arrest? You would expect an honest man to do that?'

'In theory.'

'But in fact he might weaken?'

'Who can tell?'

I was reluctant to commit myself to this way out. I certainly could not attempt it more than once, and if it were to come unstuck, I would be in fearsome trouble. Moreover, the more innocuous my false arrest, the more likely the manoeuvre was to fail. I could, for example, without much difficulty concoct a *prima facie* case against Florence Belfield, perhaps without too much harm done. But might not our honest murderer be prepared to write Florence Belfield off, at her age and in her state of mind, without much more than a wrinkle on his integrity? It depended on what he meant by integrity. Whatever Esmond Fuller might say about standards of truth, an honest murderer stepping forward to claim his death penalty must surely struggle through some coils of casuistry first. He – or she – might consider even Gilbert Slack expendable. A conscience looking anxiously round for narcotics might easily let itself be persuaded that Gilbert Slack's was the deepest moral guilt for all that had happened at Dead-Nettle.

I could so easily pull Slack in, on the mainly nugatory count of deliberately misleading us. But would that be enough? It would be uppermost in everyone's mind that a more serious charge was pending. Wouldn't my man just sit tight until it actually materialised? Or didn't?

Isobel's aunt came into the room. 'I think that that man has been up there long enough,' she said.

That was what she had to think. Things had been going on long enough which she had not even been invited to control. She looked at Fuller and me in turn for decision. Neither of us answered her.

We were on the brink, I felt, of an irrelevant interchange. But I saw the door-handle turn — we had heard nobody outside — and Lomas pushed open the door for Isobel to precede him into the room. She was wearing a grey cashmere dressing-gown, not new, her hair was loosely tied in a ribbon at the nape of her neck, and her face was as pale as I had expected it to be. Weak after days in bed, she was uncertain of her balance.

Lomas bore the look of a raw amateur actor concentrating fiercely and in near panic on the lines he had learned, waiting his delayed cue to say them, knowing that his confidence would support him once he had heard the sound of his own voice. They were a couple who had made up their minds on the most fundamental issue in their lives. And in view of what was going to happen within the next few minutes, it was right that they should have done so. Every shred of decency and humanity within me demanded that I should leave them alone with Fuller for a short space of time. I even played with the idea of taking Aunt Dorothy out for quite unnecessary questioning. But I took myself firmly in hand. I must not miss a nuance. We even had to suffer Aunt Dorothy.

'Are you still here?' Isobel Fuller asked me, not rudely, registering objectively a melancholy fact.

'Did you think I wouldn't be?'

'I wish you no harm, Mr Brunt. And I know you're not going to vanish.'

'Certainly I am not.'

She went round behind her father and planted a kiss on his temple. 'There is something we have to say to my father. Or, at least, Frank has. He insists on doing everything strictly according to form.'

She was certain that that would get rid of me. I had risen on her entry, and not taken seat again yet, but I stood immovable.

'In that case,' she said, 'for God's sake get it over and done with.'

She looked at me bitterly now. I was reminded of that other look on her face, on Monday morning in the ante-room amongst the crumpled linen. It was strange in this case how imprecise was all the evidence, if one dared call it that, that had prompted my most productive thinking. Horse's hooves, or no horse's hooves? Stained garments or no stained garments?

I let a silence weigh heavily on them all, but this was not entirely histrionic. My own mind was still making itself up. I deliberately opened my note-book and unscrewed the cap of my fountain-pen.

'Strictly according to form, then – '

I think it is true to say that until I actually opened my mouth again, I did not know what name it was that I was going to say. Gilbert Slack? Florence Belfield?

'Francis Lomas – '

'Oh, no!' Isobel said, and her aunt helped her into a chair.

I did not proceed. Lomas looked at me as if he did not understand. Esmond Fuller stirred irritably, and his elbow caught the misplaced wine-table.

'You're surely not going to charge him, Inspector?' he said.

'I fear I have evidence that you aren't aware of.'

I knew he was wrestling within himself. I did not want him to have time to think. Once it was out, it was out.

'Circumstantial evidence, Inspector?' he asked.

'Evidence that I'm sure a jury would find compelling.'

I must not try too hard. I must not pretend to tell him

any more. I must not risk feeding his lingering doubts. He moistened his lips. All along he had maintained the unthinkable: that here was a case where the law ought to turn a blind eye. All along, I now thought, he had intended to come forward if injustice threatened. He was that kind of man; but between the initial intention and the ultimate decision there must yawn a dark gap.

'You are looking uneasy, Mr Fuller.'

'I am trying to think.'

He was a man who claimed to have lost everything; but in this moment he could see all that he had not yet lost.

'I'm sorry about this, Lomas,' I said. 'You are a man whom I have grown to like. It is moments like this that make a police officer wish he had chosen some other calling. But – '

'Stop!'

I could see that Fuller's struggle was now as much a physical as an emotional one. His breathing, his pulse rate, his blood pressure, were all out of rhythm.

'Yes, Mr Fuller?'

'I told you, didn't I, that my alibi for Sunday night was a very imperfect one? You saw fit to see that as a strength rather than a weakness. You implied that that gave it credibility. I told you I had plenty of time, between Isobel going out and Cook coming in with my glass of warm milk, to ride over to Dead-Nettle Drift. I went there with the intention of killing that woman – but it was all academic, really. I had not actually pictured myself committing the act. It was when I saw her, tearing away at the walls of that cottage, that I *realised* her: I knew then how callous and casual she was. I saw what was true behind the tales that Slack had tried to get me to believe. I picked up one of Frank Lomas's wedges – '

Isobel was gazing with conscious fixation at a spot on the carpet.

'So how am I going to convince you that this is no confession of convenience, Inspector?'

I needed no such persuasion; but material evidence was always grist to the mill.

'Your riding-clothes, perhaps,' I said.

'You are a smart man, Inspector. And I have a smart daughter. It was my hose-tops she missed, when you made her go through my things. After that, she would not have trusted herself to go to my wardrobe. She wouldn't have found my breeches or hacking-jacket, either. But I can take you to where they are hidden. Destined for the boiler – but I haven't had the nerve to handle them again.'

He turned to the other two.

'I have a bad time coming, but you two have everything ahead of you. You'll have a bad time, too. But you'll survive.'

I walked with him across the park towards the village. There was no need to put cuffs on his wrists. We passed the absurd line of statues, all shapes and sizes and postures, drawn up like a guard-mounting parade awaiting the orderly officer. Fuller looked back over his shoulder at them and began to laugh maniacally; but not without a certain measure of self-control.

Hilton
Dead-nettle